# MYSTIFY

### *A Mystyx Novel*

# MYSTIFY

*A Mystyx Novel*

## ARTIST ARTHUR

Recycling programs
for this product may
not exist in your area.

MYSTIFY: A MYSTYX NOVEL

ISBN-13: 978-0-373-53431-9

www.KimaniTRU.com

Printed in U.S.A.

To Amaya. Always my princess.

## Acknowledgments

Thank you, Lord, for the gift.

A very special thank-you to all the bloggers who've done interviews, guest blog spots and reviews. You're the best!

To Kicheko Driggins and Lisa Roe
for your tireless work in the publicity department.

To the Kimani team——Evette Porter (editor extraordinaire),
Glenda Howard, Brie Edmonds-Ashton and Shara Alexander
for believing in the Mystyx and working so diligently
to make sure the series had a grand debut.

To Christine Witthohn for listening to me,
for giving me that kick in the butt when I needed it
and for generally being the best at what you do.

To the readers who have welcomed the Mystyx into your lives
with open arms, many, many thank-yous.

And to my family for always being
exactly what I need, when I need it.

Dear Reader,

Krystal Bentley introduced you to the Mystyx in *Manifest*. Now it's Sasha Carrington's turn to pull you completely into their world.

Sasha's life is a little out of control right now—her parents are finally paying attention to her but not in a way she wants, and she's crushing on this boy she should probably leave alone. The Darkness is also back, haunting the Mystyx and bringing with it more drama.

This second installment in the Mystyx series was fun to write, because I had the chance to do more research into a subject that has intrigued me for years—Greek mythology. There are many facets to this series, many things that you might have predicted, but even more that will come as a complete surprise. I'm enjoying the journey and hope you will, too!

Artist

*There has to be evil so that good can prove its purity above it.*

—Buddha

# one

I don't want to like him.

I really don't.

But I keep thinking about him—dreaming about him. It's like I'm obsessed with him. And I want to know everything about him, which isn't much, because I try not to talk to him more than I have to. That's been working out pretty well since we helped find his brother Ricky's killer. Of course it helped Ricky's spirit find peace and cross over after his death.

Me and my friends, Krystal and Jake—well, I should say my fellow Mystyx—we did that. That night was such a rush. When I remember it now, I get goose bumps. And sometimes I get scared all over again. There was something evil and dark living inside Mr. Lyle, the biology teacher, something that Jake, Krystal and I believe might still be here in Lincoln.

Lincoln, Connecticut, which is where we live, is probably one of the most boring towns there is. Nothing even remotely exciting happens here. The fact that Mr. Lyle was running an underage porn ring was the most shocking thing around here in a long time.

Now the only thing that's on people's minds is the weather. It snowed twenty-seven inches the first week of May. Then, as if Mother Nature wanted to apologize, seven days after the first snowfall, it got so hot the temperature went up to ninety-eight degrees with sixty percent humidity. (I know this because Krystal's boyfriend, Franklin—his father is the local weatherman. Franklin gives her weather updates all the time, and she tells me and Jake.)

Today the snow is just about gone. The sun's still shining, and it's really warm outside. But there are lots of puddles because of the melting snow.

But that's getting off track. I was thinking about the boy I don't like, or rather trying not to think about him, because I don't like him.

I breathe out heavily, making the hair in my face flutter. It doesn't change reality though. And the reality is that I *do* like Antoine Watson, even though I know I shouldn't.

It's not just the class differences that, for the record, are a big deal here in Lincoln. There're other reasons why me and Antoine don't make such a good couple.

He's into music and clothes and hangs with a hip-hop crowd. While I like—more like love—clothes and I'm not into cliques. That's why I avoid Alyssa Turner and her minions like the plague. Alyssa's fifteen, just like me. She lives in a huge house on the lake, just like all the other well-to-do families, known as the Richies in Lincoln. She has the best of everything and makes sure nobody ever forgets it. There's nothing more important in Alyssa's world than Alyssa. Get my drift?

I don't like anybody telling me who to hang with or why. Antoine doesn't seem like that. But the day I went to talk to him, two of the boys—who he later told me were named, of all things, Fats and Trigga—were rude and insulting, just because my parents have money. I didn't care enough to find out their real names because the ones Antoine used were so ridiculous I couldn't comprehend anything else. I just wanted them all to get a life. That's what Antoine calls being *stuck-up.* He's told me that a time or two. Funny how that always seems to roll off his tongue right after I turn him down for a date or refuse to give him my phone number.

See, I think Antoine's a little confused himself. At the dance—before I had to rush off with the other Mystyx—he talked differently. We actually had a decent conversation, and he danced okay until he started grinding up against me like we were in a rap video. I didn't like that at all and was relieved when Krystal pulled me away.

That said, there's no reason I should still be thinking about him. But here I am on a Friday night, lying across my bed thinking about where Antoine could be. Who he's with? What he's doing?

It's so weird.

Which is another thing, I should be getting used to being weird. I'm half South American and half—what would you call it—North American? My mother is from Buenos Aires, Argentina, and that's where she had me. She married my dad who's white and is originally from Houston, Texas, but moved to the east coast years ago.

We moved to Lincoln right after I was born and in this small town I'm probably the only Latina teenager. Krystal, who has been my friend for going on two months now, is part Native American and African-American. So I suppose we have something in common, even if it's only being weird and being mixed.

Krystal and I share something else. The *M* shaped birthmark that sits just above my right hip and the one Krystal has on the back of her neck. Jake, he's a Tracker—someone with less money who lives on the other side of the old railroad tracks— he has the same mark on his arm. We figured out that the *M* stands for Mystyx so that's what we call ourselves. We each have a supernatural ability that we think has something to do with atmospheric events that happened around the time we were conceived. That's why we listen to the weather reports Krystal gets from Franklin.

Like I said, it's weird.

To help make sense of it all, about an hour ago I sent an email to a woman who I think can help us figure out the nature of our powers. Or at least I hope she can.

Now I'm lying here waiting for my PC to beep with the sound of an incoming email, or rather, trying not to think of Antoine and the feelings I have for him.

I'm not asleep although my body feels kind of heavy like it's sinking into the mattress. My eyes are closed because I was tired of looking at the ceiling, waiting and trying not to think too much.

It really doesn't matter. The more I try not to think about him, the more his mocha complexion and smiling face appear in my mind. He is really cute, which right there is enough to make any girl like him. His dark hair is always close cropped and precisely cut like he has a barbershop in his house. His clothes, of course, are stylish, baggy jeans, oversize shirts— either button-downs or T-shirts—and black or brown boots. Most of the other guys in his crowd tend to wear too much jewelry, but Antoine only wears a chain with a cross hanging from it. His left ear is pierced and he always smells good. Antoine always wears cologne. I don't know what it's called, but I like it. I can smell it now, here in my bedroom. If I inhale deeply, the scent fills my nose, and when I exhale I want to see him even more.

I want to see him and talk to him, maybe try to figure out what this thing between us is. I figure it's probably not going to go away, and I don't know how else to deal with it.

I wonder if he likes me. I think he does because he keeps asking me out, and lately he always seems to be where I am.

I wonder what he's doing tonight, if he's home in his room thinking about me. I wonder...

Am I floating on something?

Wait a minute, I'm dizzy. It's cold in here. Did Casietta turn on the air-conditioning already?

My eyes are fluttering, trying to open. But when they finally do, I can't really believe what I'm seeing.

It's dark, really, really dark. Like pitch darkness—not like sometimes when you wake up in the middle of the night and can kind of see where things are so you don't walk into walls when you're trying to get to the bathroom. No, this is pitch blackness and it's cold, and I'm moving, going someplace.

Then as quickly as it becomes dark, it turns loud, noisy and filled with music. I jump. I mean my body jerks forward like I've just been scared awake, and I look around trying to figure out why my bedroom has changed into what looks like a nightclub.

# two

The first thing I do is pinch myself. Ow! Okay, that hurt.

Next I close my eyes, take a deep breath, then open them again.

I'm still here, still standing against the wall at a club. From the gold–and–black lettering on the wall across the room, behind and just above the DJ booth, I see that I'm in Trends. It's a nightclub for the eighteen to twenty-five crowd that's only open on Wednesday and Thursday nights. On Friday it's free for all before midnight. I look down at my watch and notice that it's a few minutes until then. I'm not eighteen, so I definitely don't want to be caught in here.

My parents would flip if that happened. Not that they pay much attention to me. But I'm thinking that something like this might turn their heads and not in a good way.

It hasn't escaped me that a few minutes ago I was lying on my bed, in my room, on the other side of town. No, I realize that something has just happened, something most likely related to my ability to move my body with my mind. One thing I know for certain is that our Mystyx powers will grow. It's just that we don't know in what way. Something tells me I'm getting a preview of mine right now.

But why here? Why now?

Two seconds later I have the answer.

"You sure are fine, Sasha, even if you're out of your element here."

He walked up to me just like he knew I was going to be here, like I was waiting for him, which is so totally not true. Or is it?

"What are you doing here, Antoine?"

He laughs, his lips spreading with the smile. He's wearing exactly what I'd pictured him in, jeans, T-shirt and boots. The diamond stud—I don't know if it's real or not—in his ear sparkling with the flashing lights in the club.

"I was about to ask you the same thing." He moved fast, pushing his body right up against mine like I'd asked him to dance.

But I didn't ask him to dance, so I back up, but the wall stops my retreat. And Antoine, he just moves right along with me so that he's still up in my face.

"You look pretty tonight," he says, smiling as he looks me up and down.

It's irritating the way his eyes rake over me. Then again it's kind of flattering. I guess. I'm not wearing anything special so I don't really know why he says I look pretty. It's just jeans and a fitted T-shirt—similar to what he's wearing except my shirt is yellow and his is white. Anyway, like I said, I'm not wearing anything special because I didn't plan on being here.

"Thank you," I finally say, remembering my manners. "Ah, how long have you been here?"

What I really want to know is how exactly I came to be here, and more to the point, how long will I be able to stay?

"Since around nine, like I told you I would be. I didn't think you'd show," he says.

"What?"

"You know, I asked you at school the other day if we could go out tonight—if you wanted to hang at the club with me.

But as usual you shot me down cold. Now here you are." He shrugs like he's happy about the outcome.

Antoine's like that. No matter how many times I turn him down, he just keeps asking me out. You could call him a glutton for punishment, but I have a feeling he's something else entirely.

Still, I had forgotten all about him asking me out. I'm so used to turning him down. But it couldn't be his simple request that brought me here. I have a sinking suspicion it's much more.

"So you wanna dance, or you just wanna chill?"

My legs are starting to feel shaky. Images of my room flash before my eyes like a movie trailer. What's going on? I've been asking myself that question for years, ever since the first time I disappeared from one side of a room and reappeared on the other.

I shake my head at Antoine. I don't want to dance or chill. I want to figure out what's going on with me. "Actually, I should probably get going."

"You just got here," he replies.

Something about the way he says it nags at me, maybe because I hear the tiniest hint of disappointment in his voice. "I guess we could dance just once," I hear myself saying.

Unbelievable, I know. I have no clue how I got here from my bedroom. I've never traveled psychokinetically—that's a complicated way of saying I use my mind to move things, like my body—this far before. Yet here I am. And here is Antoine, taking my hand and pulling me to the middle of the dance floor. I notice some of the other hip-hop crowd, but try to look in the opposite direction. The music is fast with a lot of bass, some track with T-Pain because I can hear the Auto-Tune lyrics. I'm a little nervous about dancing with Antoine, again because of the last time when he was trying to go all the way with me on the dance floor.

But this time is different. Antoine starts to dance, but he isn't rubbing all up on me.

"C'mon, show me what you got, pretty girl."

He's moving in precise rhythm with the thumping bass. I can dance, a little. I mean, I don't look like I'm hearing another song inside my head than the one that's being played. I'm no video backup dancer, but I can hold my own. I know I should be thinking about how I got here right now, but instead I'm focusing on how nice Antoine looks moving to the beat.

So I begin to move and keep right on watching him. He moves closer to me only to back up again, like a choreographed dance move. I'm feeling the music and starting to feel Antoine, so the next time he dances up on me I shake my hips a little harder with my hands in the air and follow his lead. We must have looked good, like we'd practiced these moves before, because people actually back up, giving us a lot of space on the dance floor as they watch.

Normally I'm not one to make a spectacle of myself, but I feel different here with Antoine. Is it because I'm in a real club for the first time in my life? Or because I'm with Antoine? I don't really want to know the answer, not right now.

By the time the song finally ends I'm winded and laughing. Antoine's smiling and putting an arm around my waist, leading me back toward the side of the club we'd come from.

"Okay, okay, you got skills on the dance floor. I'll give you that."

He's talking like he's surprised, and I try not to be offended. It hasn't totally escaped me that I'm probably the only non-black person in this entire club. "You're not bad yourself," I respond.

"We must have looked good together. You see all the people staring at us?"

I nod, feeling a rush of something I've never felt before. "Yeah, I saw them."

"So what do you want to do now?"

I want to go home and figure out what's going on.

I want to dance with Antoine again.

But what I really want is not to like him because we're just *too* different. I don't know why this keeps coming up, but it does.

And yet, when he uses a finger to push back some of my hair, touching the skin of my cheek softly, I shiver, then feel my body warm.

"I should probably go home."

"When are you gonna stop runnin' from me?" he asks, all serious like.

I frown. "I'm not running from you. I'm not. That's just silly. I'm here, aren't I?" *Even though I still don't know how that came to be.* Suddenly, now that I'm standing still and not swaying to the beat with Antoine, my knees are feeling a little shaky again. I'm looking at Antoine, but I'm seeing the yellow walls of my room. And in the distance I can hear my mother calling my name.

This is not good. Even though I don't know what's going on, I know these images and voices are not in sync with standing in this club with Antoine.

"You know what? I have to go to the bathroom."

Antoine nods like he knows what I'm saying is a lie. Right about now I don't care. My mother's voice is growing louder in my head, and joining her is Casietta, our housekeeper, who practically raised me. They're calling me like they can't find me or I won't answer, one or the other, or maybe both.

The weakness in my legs is getting worse, so I pull away

from Antoine's grasp, quickly pushing through the crowd. All I can think of is getting into the bathroom in time. Something tells me I need to hurry before whatever is going on becomes public.

Pushing frantically through the bathroom door, I walk down the narrow walkway bending over to see if I can find an empty stall, my heart pounding. Bingo! The handicapped stall is empty. Just like in school, nobody ever goes into the bigger stall. Tonight, however, I think this is probably just the place for me.

Slamming the door and clicking the latch to lock it, I lean against the wall. My breath is coming quicker, like I've been running for miles. Closing my eyes and trying to steady my breathing, I can see more of my room—my white desk, the yellow-and-white satin valance at my window.

Then I'm in the dark. In the cool again, floating. I'm moving fast, a breeze tickling my cheeks. I can't see a thing, but I know I'm somewhere else, somewhere in between.

I jerk, my body shaking abruptly. I sit up, then fall right back down onto the softness.

"Sasha? Sasha?"

That's my mom's voice.

*"Son usted bien, la princesa?"*

Casietta is asking if I'm all right in Spanish and calling me by the nickname she always uses. She says I was born the princess of the Carrington household. When I was younger I used to love to pretend I was just that—*la princesa*. I pretended to live in a castle and had lots of pretty things. But I've long since grown out of the name, long since gotten over all the pretty things in my big, pretty house. I don't have the heart to tell Casietta that.

Slowly my eyes open again, although I'm not sure if I'm

gonna see the club and Antoine's smiling face again or that eerie darkness. It's blurry at first. Then I see two faces and almost scream. Not because of the faces—no. Casietta has the same olive-toned skin with raven black hair tinged with gray pulled back into a neat bun. My mom's face is the same too. Her skin is just a shade lighter than Casietta's—probably because of her makeup—with her long, dark, shiny hair that hangs past her shoulders. She's wearing her diamond studs. The Ladies Auxiliary, that's where she has been. She always wears her diamond stud earrings to the meetings.

I want to scream because I'm right back in my room. Just two minutes ago I was dancing at Trends with Antoine.

"When did you two come in?" is the first thing that comes out of my mouth.

Lidia Carrington and Casietta exchange curious looks. Then Casietta, with her hand already plastered across my forehead, asks, "Are you feeling okay?"

"She looks a little pale," my mom adds.

"No fever," Casietta says as I move out of her reach.

"I'm not sick," I say, sitting up straight in the bed. The movement makes the room shift right in front of me, and I feel like I just stepped off a Ferris wheel. I'm rethinking my declaration of not being sick because my stomach does feel a bit queasy.

"Was I lying here when you came in?" I'm more comfortable talking to Casietta than I am to my own mother, so my question is directed to her.

"Of course you were, *princesa*. What is wrong with you? You sleep like the dead."

Closing my eyes, my throat clenches as I try to swallow her words. Sleeping like the dead, that's what she'd said. That meant I hadn't left this room. But I had been in the club.

Maybe I was sick or sleeping so soundly that I really dreamt the whole scene at Trends.

Yeah, that makes sense.

"Well, get up and get yourself together," my mother says, already moving from my side and smoothing out the knee-length linen skirt she's wearing. "Your father's waiting for us in the den."

"Us?" I'm asking because my father, Marvin Carrington, never waits for me. He's up every morning before I get up for school and doesn't usually come home at night until I'm in bed. Weekends are no different. I don't see him at breakfast or dinner or anything in between. I know his comings and goings only because his black Jaguar is either in the garage or not. My mother isn't much better. As a member of one of Lincoln's wealthiest families, she has important stuff to do during the day. Not like a paying job—that would be so beneath her. No, Lidia holds the position of either chairperson or cochair of every social club in town. If it's a high-class or high-minded cause, Lidia is on it. From the Ladies Auxiliary to the Women's Society, even to the despicable Mothers of Debutantes Committee, Lidia's a key member. All these causes and committees keep her away from the house and me, her only child, more often than not.

"Yes, dear—us. Now, get up and wash your face. And what are you wearing?"

Casietta is already helping me out of the bed, biting her tongue as she often does when my mother is around. Sometimes I get the feeling Casietta doesn't approve of the things my mother does or doesn't do. But she's never spoken a bad word about her, probably because my mother brought Casietta with her from Buenos Aires when she left. I guess that means Casietta owes my mother some kind of debt. But I assume that raising her daughter and managing the Carrington household staff for the last sixteen years should be payment enough. I could be wrong though.

"I'm wearing clothes, Mom," I say, knowing it sounds like I've got attitude, but I don't care.

Nothing I do is ever good enough for my mother. I mean, on the rare occasion that she remembers I'm alive and still living in this house, she usually doles out more criticism than compliments.

"I don't know why you insist on wearing those jeans all the time. You're a young lady, you should dress like one."

"I'm a teenager. Jeans and a T-shirt are the staple of my daily wardrobe," I quip, standing on wobbly legs but nodding Casietta away.

I still think something weird is going on. But I want to check my laptop to see if I've gotten an email. Halfway across the room, my mother interrupts me by clearing her throat loudly.

"The bathroom is that way, Sasha."

I feel like shouting I know where the bathroom is, but Casietta doesn't stand for backtalk, so I try to keep it to a minimum—when I can.

"I just need to check my email real quick."

"No. We don't have a lot of time. I didn't think we'd have to spend so much time trying to wake you. We've kept your father waiting long enough. Now I'm going down. I expect to see you in five minutes."

She's already walking toward the door. Not giving me a chance to respond as usual. Sighing at the things that will never change, I'm already moving across the room to my desk, quickly flipping open my laptop.

Once my mother leaves the room, Casietta speaks up. "Your papa will be steaming mad if you do not hurry up."

I shrug. "That would be the first emotional reaction I've ever seen from him. Might be interesting."

"Watch your mouth, *princesa*. They are still your parents." Casietta mumbles something as she smoothes the comforter on my bed.

I'm curious what else she has to say but more concerned with an answer to my email.

To: princesssasha@lincolnmail.ing
From: wiccangoddess@cnettrix.ing
Re: Witch Trials

Hold your letter up to the light. Email me back with what you see.

Cryptic.

Then again, nothing dealing with these powers or this so-called Darkness is easy to explain. Still, at least she responded to me. Now all I need to do is get the letter from Jake's great grandmother's journal, the one that was written by Mary Burroughs who was accused of being a witch and burned during the Salem Witch Trials. Mary wasn't a witch, I'm convinced of that. She was a Mystyx just like me, and I'm going to prove it and find out just how many more of us there are out there and why we exist.

Krystal and Jake think the origin of the Mystyx is steeped in Greek mythology. Like the Olympians and the Titans, Zeus and Aphrodite. Personally, I think our power comes more from the Wiccan beliefs. I came to that conclusion after we found Jake's grandmother's journal. Mary Burroughs also had a power, one that was misunderstood. Me, Krystal and Jake decided to keep our powers a secret. But I don't leave anything to chance if I can help it. So I'm thinking ahead, protecting us and our powers before others find out and reenact a modern-day witch hunt.

But first I have to deal with my parents. I'm sure whatever they want is just as superficial and materialistic as their lifestyle. But since I've got to live here another two years until I'm eighteen, I'll have to go with the flow.

# three

"The Oaks Center will be an exclusive club for only the elite members of Lincoln's society."

My father is talking—*the* Marvin Carrington, with his tall broad shoulders and silver-gray hair. He's forty-five years old, three years older than my mother. He was born in Houston and inherited some of his father's oil money. Using his inheritance, he started his own company, Carrington Investments. From what I can tell, people pay him money to invest their money. If all goes well, they both get richer. I guess that's the name of the game for everybody these days.

Anyway, he's been talking for the last fifteen minutes. I made it downstairs in about seven minutes, which had my mother shooting daggers at me with her eyes. If there's one thing she hates, it's making my father angry. Me, I don't care how they feel about me at this point. Still, I guess any show of emotion from them is better than nothing.

"So I'd like to have my girls behind me in this venture," my father says, finishing up.

I'm barely paying attention.

"Of course, Marvin. Sasha and I will do whatever we have to. This venture will be a success just like everything else the Carrington name is behind."

Blah, blah, blah. I hear the sound of their voices, but my

mind keeps going back to the email, the letter, the strange trip to the club. And of course, Antoine.

"Sasha?"

My father's heavy voice pulls me out of the other world I usually live in—the one where parents aren't allowed or *tolerated*, I should say.

"Yes, sir?" I stumble over the words and clasp my hands in front of me. He's staring at me. That makes me uncomfortable since I'm not used to being in the same room with him.

"You'll have a special assignment in this venture."

"Me? What do you want me to do?"

"I'll need you to help recruit young people. I want the Oaks Center to include the affluent younger generation and pave the way for the future. We won't exclude them this time, but rather teach our values."

*Our values,* like we're a separate species or something. The confused and more than slightly irritated expression on my face must be evident, because my mother clears her throat.

"Sasha can do that. There are a lot of students in her school, even in her class, that she can help recruit. Right, Sasha?"

*Recruit? What am I, some type of employee?* "Ah, I don't know."

One of my father's bushy eyebrows arches. I guess this is his intimidating look. I can see some of the people who work for him becoming nervous, but I don't see this look often, so I'm not sure how to react.

My mother, as diplomatically as she possibly can, moves quickly across the room and is at my side before I can say another word. Wrapping her arm around me, she digs her fingers into my shoulder. I try not to cringe. "She'll do just fine, Marvin. I'll work with her personally."

His one eyebrow lowers, and his lips thin into a straight line. He nods, then turns toward the bar and picks up a glass.

"Very good. We're having a cocktail party. Everyone who is anyone in Lincoln will be here. We want them all on board with this venture."

He's still talking. Since I'm clearly not interested in what he's saying, I look toward the window. My mother is still standing next to me holding me close like she thinks that's going to make a difference, like her firm grip can make me listen or obey.

She doesn't have a clue.

Astrology is my thing. Not many people know that. Well, okay, nobody knows that. It's my secret, even though I really don't know why I keep it a secret. It's not like I'm a nerd or anything. I just like the stars. When I was seven, my father hired someone to paint my ceiling like the night sky with the stars in the shape of my favorite constellation, Orion. When I turned fourteen I figured I was too old for that and repainted my room a pale yellow. It suited my mood at the time. Right now, even though it's morning, my mood is like the night sky, dark and starry, drifting, yet clearly a part of something.

"Something" meaning whatever is going on with the Mystyx. And there is definitely something going on. Fatima, that's the follower of Wicca who I researched online and contacted, and who had responded to my message. But I need to get to Jake's house and the journal to figure out what her message means.

What I know right now, as I'm sitting in the back of the car while Mouse—my larger-than-life driver—takes me to school is that we've pinpointed the origin of our powers to cataclysmic weather events and the mythical Greek river, Styx. But I feel like there's so much more we're missing—like how is the weather connected to the River Styx? And the power, it comes from powerful energy emitted during major storms. It just isn't adding up.

My mind flashes back to the stars and how I sometimes feel just as distant from my family as they are from the earth. I know enough about astrology to know that the Greeks believed in the power of the moon and the sun. They believed the sun to be the manifestation of the god Apollo, and the moon, with its three distinct phases—full, quarter and half—was linked to three goddesses—the maiden Artemis, the motherly Selene and Hecate, the goddess of the Underworld. Somehow, it all fits together with the idea that the sun dominates the sky during the day, thus representing vitality and life, while the moon comes into its power at night, bringing fertility, nurturing and the perpetuation of the cycle of life and death. The knowledge that the moon really has eight lunar phases probably wasn't known to the Greeks at the time.

Still, I think there's a correlation. I feel like the moon might explain a significant part of our power—or at the very least, my power.

Arriving in front of the school, I figure I should probably shift my mind to the classroom. Good grades aren't hard for me. But with all this going on, I don't want to take anything for granted.

Just as I step out of the car, I see Krystal and Franklin getting off the school bus. They instantly hold hands and walk side by side into the school building. I wonder how that feels. To be a part of a couple, I mean. I can do that, I'm sure, be a girlfriend to some guy. Question is, do I want that guy to be Antoine?

# four

The next two days are spent keeping an eye out for Antoine, who I finally decide I don't want to see. Being with him in that club was surely a dream, one I hadn't revisited since that night, thankfully.

I resigned myself to forget how real or how right it felt to be with Antoine. Both were totally unbelievable.

Now I'm anxious to go to lunch to see Jake and Krystal. While I have no intention of telling them about my goofy Antoine dream, I've been impatiently waiting to see the journal again. When I'd called Jake on Saturday morning to tell him that I was coming over to look at the journal, he must have had some stuff going on because he kind of stuttered and gave me like five different reasons why that wasn't possible.

Jake's home life is anything but smooth sailing. His grandfather is really cool, if you don't count the days he doesn't know his name and forgets to put on his pants. His father, on the other hand, always seems angry, on the days that he stays home long enough for me or Jake to see him. It's for that reason alone that I decide to just send Jake a text this morning asking him to bring the journal to school.

Heading to the cafeteria I look around one more time just to make sure Antoine and his crew aren't around. I can't believe how lucky I've been not to run into him for this long. Still, I don't want to tempt fate, so I hurry into the cafeteria and sit at the table Jake, Krystal and I usually occupy.

"So I was thinking we should meet tonight, at the library," Jake says while chewing the biggest bite of a hotdog I'd ever seen. His cheek looks like he stuck a golf ball inside his mouth, and I sigh in disgust.

Krystal, who just started eating like a normal teenager a couple of weeks ago, shakes her head in agreement. I think Krystal is going through a lot with her mom. In the first few weeks we'd known each other, I figured she just had the regular teenage woes that all of us have. But turns out hers are a little different. Krystal's real father is a real idiot. He cheated on Krystal's mother with the nanny—how clichéd. Then he got the nanny pregnant and moved to the West Coast to be with her. Krystal was stuck here in Lincoln, a small, behind-the-times town, with her mother and her stepfather. I don't think either one of them is that bad, but then I don't have to live with them.

From the outside looking in, people probably think Lidia and Marvin Carrington are the best parents a girl could have—they work all the time and give me about as much attention as they do the other furniture in the house. They make sure I'm always dusted and shined to perfection when guests come to the house. Otherwise, I'm sort of just there.

"That's a good idea," Krystal says, her voice bringing me back to the current conversation.

"Can't," I add, chewing on yet another celery stick. My mom might not know what classes I'm taking this semester or my favorite color, but she knows what size clothes I wear and will bust a button in her designer suits if she finds out I'm eating anything other than health food.

"C'mon, Sasha," Jake whines. "This is important. You remember Krystal's vision. It's coming for us, for everybody."

Krystal is a medium. She can see, hear and talk to ghosts. And just recently we found out that she has visions. However, we aren't all that sure whether those visions are of the past or the future. The Darkness, that's what we call the black fog and the blackbirds that seem to always flock around us. It's some type of evil. That much we all agree on. How to fight it is the question.

"I know. I know. But my parents are having this cocktail party thing and I have to be there."

"You never go to their parties," Jake argues.

And he's right. I always try to get out of going to whatever gatherings my parents are having, because I already know I'll be bored out of my mind. Not to mention they never care if I'm there or not. But a couple weeks ago, right around the time we came into our powers and this freaky dark cloud started surrounding us, my mom started asking me questions about some of the kids at school. Other Richies, of course, because those are the only people my parents care about. The other day I found out *why* they've been asking all those questions. They want me to be some kind of recruiter of the rich kids at school for this new exclusive club they are starting. I don't want to be bothered, but don't really have a choice.

"Look, I just have to be at this thing with them or they'll freak. So Jake, did you bring the journal?"

"Yeah," he answers, taking another bite of food. He pulls it out of his backpack and pushes it across the table to me. "What do you need it for? We've all read it over and over again and agreed there aren't any new clues in there."

I was already flipping through the pages, looking for the letter. "I've got another lead. Remember we read the letter from Mary Burroughs that seemed to connect us to the Salem Witch Trials."

"Mary was hanged for being a witch," Krystal said.

I nodded. "But I don't think she was a witch at all. I think she was a Mystyx."

"You've said that before."

Then I find the letter and gingerly pull it out of the book. The paper is very thin and fragile, like it would crumble into pieces at any moment. I lift my arms, tilting back so that the letter is in a direct line with the fluorescent light.

"Wow," I sigh as I spy what I suspect Fatima wanted me to see.

"What are you doing?"

I look at Jake and Krystal. "I found this practicing wiccan online. She lives in Bridgeport. Anyway, I asked her a couple of questions about our powers and I told her about the journal we found. She wrote back and told me to hold the letter up to the light and to get back to her with what I saw."

Jake frowns. Krystal put down her soda can. "And what do you see?"

"Look for yourself," I say, handing them the letter.

Since I already read it I'm mulling over the possible meanings. It reads:

**In another time, in another place, power reigns supreme over the entire race.**
**Yet some were bold, resisting the warnings told.**
**Now the dark rises amongst innocent cries and only those bathed in the light shall break the ties.**

Behind the written words is a watermark—the letter *M*, which looks exactly like our birthmarks.

"I don't get it," Jake says.

Krystal looks as confused as I am. "Did you see the *M?*"

"I saw it," Jake says, "but I still don't get it."

"A curse? Maybe the Darkness that's following us is the curse?" I add.

"So now we have a letter from a witch, powers connected to a storm and a curse," says Krystal, and she's getting that faraway look she gets when she's thinking. "What else did the witch say?"

"She said to get back to her with what I found on the back of this letter."

Jake nods. "So you email her back and tell her. But how do you know she's safe?"

"Because nothing I'm saying so far is credible. No one will believe her," I quip. "Look, Jake, I know you're afraid of people finding out we have powers and the repercussions of that. But right now, nobody is even aware of anything being wrong around here. I'm just trying to get us some answers. The more we know about why we have these powers, the better we'll be able to fight whatever is after us."

"I agree," Krystal says. "Email her tonight and see what she says. Then tomorrow we definitely need to go to the library to see what we can find about curses in Greek mythology."

"Why about Greek mythology?" I ask, because I'm thinking that maybe the witch in Bridgeport can give us some answers.

"Because it says that the heroes are bathed in the water and in the light. The River Styx," she says waiting for us to catch on.

"The heroes are bathed in the river?" Jake asks. "That's not possible. The river circled the Underworld serving as the border between earth and the Underworld. It was like some sort of black ash. Nobody could swim through that."

Krystal shakes her head. "Not true. Achilles's mother dipped him into the River Styx. Every part of him except the heel of his foot, and it made him invulnerable to every place the water touched."

I shake my head, not satisfied with this explanation. "But we weren't even living during the time of the River Styx. How could this relate to us and our powers in today's world?"

"I don't know," Krystal says. "But there's got to be a way— genetics or something."

"I doubt my family tree goes back to the Greek gods," I say, taking the letter from Jake.

"Mine either. Still, it opens another door. We should check it out," he says.

Jake closes the journal and puts it back in his bag.

Krystal is nodding in agreement. "Okay, tomorrow it is. My mother wants me to go to Bible study tonight anyway."

"Bible study!" Jake frowns. "I didn't know you went to church."

"We used to. I mean, my grandmother on my father's side always made me go when we visited her. And my mother joined a church when we were in New York. We haven't been since moving here. But she started going like two weeks ago and really wants me to join her."

"Great, your parents are dragging you to church and mine are dressing me up to smile and play nice at a party. I really wish they'd get a clue."

"Who doesn't like a party?" Lindsey Yi chimes in. She's the new girl at Settleman's High. She joins our table and immediately starts talking.

We met Lindsey the night of the spring dance. That night she was hitting on Jake like he was drenched in honey and she was queen bee. The memory of how exasperated Jake looked as Lindsey was gyrating her body against him still made me giggle.

Ever since that night, Lindsey has been popping up wherever

we are, which probably isn't a good thing because, with all the freaky stuff going on around us, she might see something she doesn't understand. Although, I swear, the girl never stops talking long enough to see anything other than the words coming out of her mouth.

Case in point, she's still chattering away even though none of us have said hello or gotten a word in edgewise.

"At my last school we had a dance every month. There was always a theme to the dances like a masquerade ball, a black-and-white party, a slumber party. Like I said, everybody loves to party. I don't get that Lincoln is like that, though. Seems a little more uptight here than it was in Milan." She shrugs. "Guess that might be a cultural thing."

I almost choke trying to swallow my bottled water. Did she just say a "cultural" thing? I'm pretty sure she's Chinese. I'm half Argentinean. Jake's white and Krystal's part Native American, part African-American. Could our little table be any more diverse?

"It's a private party," Jake says in a tone that's unlike him. Lindsey makes him uncomfortable. I wonder if that means he likes her—I mean, *likes* her.

"Just a little get-together that my parents are having," I say, trying to defuse the tension. Even though Lindsey doesn't look like she's bothered by what Jake says at all.

She just waves a hand as if dismissing Jake altogether. "That's fine. I was just saying that we used to have parties all the time. Anyway, what else do you guys do around here to have fun?"

Fun? In Lincoln? Was there any? Not that I can think of.

When nobody answers right away, Lindsey just shrugs. "I understand how you feel, Sasha."

"What?" I say because I haven't said anything, and I'm totally lost as to what she's talking about.

"You don't want to go to the party, don't want to be bothered with your parents and their fake friends. Actually, it's still a mystery to you why they even want you there."

And how did she know all that? "Ah, yeah, I guess," I say, stumbling over my words as I stare at her.

She's short, I mean shorter than both me and Krystal, which means she's got to be like five feet two or three inches. Her hair is long and jet black and hangs straight down her back. Her bangs are cut stylishly long so that it looks like she can barely see. Yet she's looking at me as if she can see right through me. Strange.

The bell rings, and Jake quickly jumps up from the table first. "Gotta go," he says but then waits for Krystal to get up.

But as Krystal gets up, we're joined by another student. I'd been wondering where Franklin was. After the spring dance he'd almost become a member of our little clique.

Franklin Bryant is Krystal's boyfriend now. Most lunch periods Franklin sits with us, his arm around Krystal's chair while Jake watches them both out of the corner of his eye. Now Jake's frowning as Franklin's arm—as expected—snakes around Krystal's shoulder.

"Hey, ready for afternoon classes?" Franklin asks in that geeklike voice of his. He's not really a geek just because his father is the local weatherman, and he talks about storms and high pressure fronts more than anything else. I guess they make a cute couple.

"Not at all," Krystal says, smiling and grabbing her books. "I've got American History with Alyssa Turner."

Lindsey opens her mouth and sticks a finger inside like she's gagging. "I don't know what's worse, history or Alyssa."

Alyssa Turner is the resident *bitch* at Settleman's High. She hates any- and everyone who doesn't live in Sea Point, the neighborhood where all the other Richies live. Because I live only two doors down from her, I guess that puts me square on her BFF list. Woo-hoo, for me.

"I've got Chemistry," I say, smiling at Lindsey. She's different from anyone else in Lincoln. And I don't know why, but I'm starting to like her.

"Oh," Franklin says, pausing.

He and Krystal are walking in front of me and Lindsey. Jake is lagging behind me. So when Franklin stops, all of us stop.

"Did you guys hear about the kids that are missing?"

Krystal immediately frowns. "No. What are you talking about?"

Franklin sort of shrugs. "I just got a tweet on Twitter," he says motioning toward his cell phone that's stuck in his front pocket. "It just said that this bus from Pennsylvania full of kids on some kind of religious retreat was due back two days ago. None of the parents have talked to their kids and the bus driver last checked in with the bus company on Friday afternoon."

"That's way weird," Lindsey says in a quiet tone. She's holding her books in one hand, but the other hand moves to her temple where her fingers are massaging. "I hope they're all right."

The second warning bell rings, and we all start walking to class. At first, everything seems routine just like any other school day. Except I know it isn't. I feel it deep inside. I have a sick sense that nothing is ever going to be the same again.

# five

The dining room and half the veranda that wraps around the first floor of our house had been transformed while I was at school. Mouse brought me straight home as per my mom's instructions. Coming through the front door, I hear the sound of crystal clinking as the caterers prepare for the party.

There are at least twenty people dressed in black pants and black polo shirts with the catering company logo milling around the house. Strangers, is all I can think, as I bypass my usual trip to the kitchen for a snack. Casietta always has something for me to eat after school, something that isn't precisely on my mom's list of healthy diet food. Hey, I'm all for healthy, but every once in a while I'd like to eat something that really tastes good.

My mother's ban on any food that's remotely appealing is killing me. I love cheeseburgers, absolutely adore them. Casietta knows this, and at least twice a month she makes sure she fixes one especially for me. In Casietta's mind, if she fixes it, there's no way it can be unhealthy. Now, I don't know exactly what she puts into it, but it's pretty good. However, nothing beats a value meal, which Jake and I order most of the times we visit the one and only mall near Lincoln.

Today I'll have to forgo the snack. My mom's home. I hear her voice trilling through the rooms downstairs. She's giving orders, making arrangements, all the things she does best. I'm going to my room. In less than four hours I have to put on this stupid outfit she purchased and go downstairs to mingle with people I barely know and probably won't like. I guess I shouldn't say that since I really don't know who's coming to this party. Lincoln's rich and famous is what Mom had said. The classy and elite is what Dad called them. I'm thinking they're probably all stuck-up and snooty and boring as hell.

I slam my door closed and drop my books to the floor. Homework is a thought, but I can usually do that in the car on the way to school. I just plop down on my bed staring up at the ceiling instead. Before long, it's time to shower and change my clothes. I do this reluctantly, moving as slow as I possibly can, until ultimately, it's time to go and get this night over with.

So this is it. Taking the stairs one at a time, I cringe at the sound the black taffeta hoopskirt is making. After putting it on, I realized it didn't look as bad on me as it did hanging on the closet door. I think it's the extended one-inch hem of turquoise crinoline that peeks from beneath the dark skirt that stops just below my knees. Still, it's noisy. The blouse is a wraparound, turquoise, of course. My mom's great at coordinating outfits. That's probably why my closet is overflowing with clothes. That's one gene I can proudly say I've inherited from her. I like shopping for clothes too. And since there isn't much else to do in Lincoln, I spend a lot of time shopping online or from catalogs. A couple times a year, my mother goes to the city with my father and brings back carloads full of clothes, but I've never gone with her. I've never been out of Lincoln, not since they brought me here when I was a little baby.

I don't have any more time to think about clothes or what's outside of Lincoln. Guests have already started to arrive. I see two couples stepping into the front door, Casietta dressed in her best pressed black-and-white uniform, dutifully taking the women's wraps and directing people toward the dining room.

My parents are going to freak. They wanted me downstairs and by their side with a polite smile on my face at ten minutes after seven. It's now seven thirty-five. I was dressed at seven o'clock and purposely waited in my room, wondering if either one of them would come to get me. Obviously not.

Ignoring Casietta's warning glare, I fall in step behind the two couples. The men are older with salt-and-pepper colored hair. The women are older too but more vain about admitting it, so their faces are pinched and lifted and tucked. They've definitely paid their plastic surgeons a bundle of money. The one lady has a deep V in her dress showing more cleavage than should be legally allowed at her age because, while the silicone breasts are plump and riding high, the liver spots marching across her collar bone are kind of disgusting in contrast.

They're already whispering, probably about the house and all the expensive paintings and furniture. That's exactly what my parents want. It's kind of sickening to think I come from two such shallow people, but I guess we don't get to pick and choose our creators.

That thought has me thinking back to the Mystyx, which seems to be a constant on my mind lately. There's so much I don't know about this power I have. So much I want, no, actually *need* to know. I feel like there's this part of me that's foreign, like another person or entity entirely lives inside of me. For that reason alone I have to find answers to my questions or risk losing my mind.

I'm drawn to the moon. I know this. I've always been drawn to the moon. I wonder if that means something.

"Sasha! I'm soooo glad you're here. The thought of having

to go through this entire evening alone with the adults was frightening."

The sound of her voice could probably be judged as equally scary. Of course I don't say that out loud. Instead, I turn in her direction, giving the best smile I can muster.

"Hey, Alyssa. Glad you could come."

Lie.

Well, not exactly. I mean Alyssa Turner is an okay girl, if you're into her type, which I'm not generally. Still, we're the same age and like some of the same things, i.e. shopping, shoes and handbags. But I think that's where our interests end. In the last few months, Alyssa has shown her truest snobbish colors. She's absolutely obsessed with keeping the social wars alive and kicking in Lincoln. While, I think social and any other type of segregation is straight B.S.!

Other than her obsession with who should sit where and who is and is not worthy of her company, Alyssa could be cool at times. I'm probably remembering more of our middle school days than the time we've been at Settleman's because it seems like our progression into high school inflated her head just a little more—if that were even possible.

The visual of Alyssa's inflated head makes my smile more genuine. Her long micro-braided hair is pulled and stacked high on top her head tonight with a few loose strands, I guess to give a softer look to the hairdo. It's okay, I mean I think braids are nice. Except on Alyssa they seem to give her the impression that she's a goddess instead of just wearing the styled goddess braids that she purchased at the Hair Gallery in the mall.

"That outfit looks divine on you."

Are you kidding—"divine"? What fifteen-year-old says that? "Thanks," I say because it's polite. "You look nice, too."

Now that's true, and it is most of the time. Despite her

personality flaws, Alyssa definitely has a flair for fashion. Her dress is name brand—I know that for sure even though I don't know the name exactly. It's just that if it doesn't have a name, Alyssa doesn't wear it. Her dress is a little too snug for my tastes but hugs her curves that look years older than her fresh fifteen. It's purple with cap sleeves and about a three-inch slit on both sides, and the hem comes just below her knees. Her shoes, again designer, probably Italian leather, are black and square-toed, so she doesn't look overly dressed, but certainly well-dressed.

"This dress is so old, but yours is just great. Hey, we should definitely hit the mall sometime. God, can you believe we have to go in there with all those boring adults? This is so lame."

She's mirroring the thoughts in my mind. The ones about this being boring and lame, not about going to the mall with her. While I'm game for shopping, I don't know that it'll be that great of an experience to go with her.

I must have had a strange look on my face because she quickly starts shaking her head, loose braids swishing around, and I think instantly of Medusa. The goddess with snakes for hair whose stare, if returned, would turn you into stone. This Greek stuff is really starting to stick in my mind.

"I didn't mean anything bad about your parents or their little open house. It's just not my idea of fun."

I realize she's talking and figure I'd better start paying a little more attention to what she's saying. "Ah, no, no problem," I say, hoping that covers it.

"So maybe we should stick together tonight," she suggests.

Out of the corner of my eye, I see my mother approaching. She's dressed all in cream, a long skirt with a split up to her knee on the side and a jacket with her diamond pelican broach on the lapel. Her dark hair has been straightened so that it's hanging down her back, held away from her face by two diamond barrettes.

"Actually," Alyssa says, moving closer to me and lowering her voice like she's about to tell me something scandalous, "I've been thinking you could help me with something."

"Something like what?" I probably shouldn't have even asked.

"I've seen you with that new girl Krystal. God, I can't stand her. She thinks she's better than everybody when she's really nothing. You know she was the reason Camy moved away."

First, what is the saying—something about the pot calling the kettle...? Second, what the hell was she talking about? Camy Sherwood and her family moved out of Lincoln about two weeks ago. Now, while I will admit that Krystal's little friendship with the ghost of Ricky Watson sort of brought the whole sordid incident to a head, Krystal certainly didn't push Camy to the brink. Camy Sherwood and her I-wanna-be-like-Alyssa attitude did that to herself. She'd started posing for nude pictures and who knew what else with that pervert teacher Mr. Lyle (who by the way is probably in some prison cell getting the same treatment he dished out to those young girls). So once again, Alyssa is way out of line.

"Krystal didn't make Camy move," I say in the most restrained voice I can manage.

"She's just such a pain. And now she's walking around with Franklin on her heels like they're some love-struck couple. It's sickening."

I shrug. Krystal and Franklin were like glued together at the hip lately. "Well, Franklin pursued her, if you must know."

She is twirling one of those braids around her finger and looking around the room as if searching for someone. "Yeah,

well, guys don't know any better. He probably took one look
at her mixed hair and got all flustered."

What did her hair have to do with anything? Alyssa is
definitely in a world of her own.

"Anyway, it's time she was brought down a notch. Put in
her rightful place, and you and I can make that happen."

I am about to say something else when we are interrupted.

"Well, look at you two, don't you look lovely," my mom
says, coming to a stop, touching one hand to my shoulder and
the other to Alyssa's.

"Hello, Mrs. Carrington," Alyssa says politely.

"Hi, Mom," I say in a tone that just doesn't match the
general excitement coming from the two of them.

"You're both just what we need. You'll be the spokespersons
for the youth of the Oaks Club."

I don't like the sound of that.

Alyssa, on the other hand, smiles prettily, her amber eyes
just about glittering with anticipation. Alyssa likes a title, and
I can tell this is going to take her ginormous ego to another
level.

"Sure, we'd love to, Mrs. Carrington. Just tell us what you'd
like us to do."

Hoping she'll say, "change your clothes and go out for a
cheeseburger" is wishful thinking.

"Well," my mom begins in her sugary sweet voice, the
one that makes me grit my teeth every time I hear it, "what
I was thinking is that you two can rally up some of your
friends. You know, get them excited about the club and all
the possibilities."

"What are the possibilities?" I ask because I still can't figure
out why our little town even needs an exclusive club.

I mean, really, there are about four thousand people living

in Lincoln. Maybe fifteen hundred of them are well off like we are. (That's just a guess because it's not like I work for the Census Bureau and actually know the statistics.) But anyway, we're a small town, in Connecticut, of all places. We're not in Beverly Hills or Dallas or any other metropolitan city. Our town sits right on the edge of Connecticut, just beneath West Haven. The larger part of the town is sided by the Atlantic Ocean and the other part runs right along the highway.

We aren't like hillbillies or anything, but we're far from the sophisticated city life. Far from being big enough to split off into specific social groups. Looking around me, I can see my point—if vocalized—will go unheeded.

"We want the youth to be involved in this venture. You are our future, after all."

Oh please, that line is so played out.

"You two will be responsible for recruiting all the teenagers in our little circle. Get them excited about the club and all that it will offer them and their futures."

Brainwash them basically, is what I figure she means.

Alyssa, on the other hand, is happier than a pig in slop, clapping her hands together and smiling enthusiastically. "That's a great idea, Mrs. Carrington. We'd love to help."

We would?

"Don't you worry about a thing. Sasha and I will start recruiting right away."

We will?

"Thanks, girls." My mom gives us another award-winning smile and leaves us alone. Finally.

But just when I'm about to turn and tell Alyssa she's crazy for agreeing to this stupid little task, I see something—or someone, I should say—that stops me cold.

I can see into the dining room, and, just as a group of adults walk away, I can see a man and a boy from school. A boy who just happens to be the boyfriend of my fellow Mystyx.

"Who's that man with Franklin?" I ask Alyssa, still wondering why Franklin Bryant would be here in the first place.

Alyssa follows my gaze. "Oh, that's his dad. Don't you recognize him from television? He does the weather on channel eight."

That's right, he does. Walter Bryant is the local meteorologist, and he and about three or four other reporters at the station are the closest thing Lincoln has to TV stars. But what is he doing here? I'm sure that even though he's on TV, he's not making Hollywood-type money, which is exactly what the other guests of this party and the hopeful sponsors of the club are.

"My mom said he was only invited so we could get some free publicity. He was at my house a couple nights ago talking to my dad about this research project he's working on. I was supposed to be studying in the den but I could hear them through the walls. Mr. Bryant's working on some type of research project, something about really strange weather events and the impact on the environment."

Unknowingly, Alyssa answers my question and piques my curiosity. I wonder if Krystal knows about this project. Maybe she's already started pumping Franklin for information about it.

Alyssa keeps right on talking like she's having this conversation all by herself. "Plus I think Mr. Bryant's father was connected with the government or something like that. He might really be kind of famous in an off sort of way. You know, useful but not really belonging."

My neck hurts when I turn to stare at her quickly. Her last remark reminds me why I don't really like hanging with her or this crowd of people my parents want so desperately to be around. So I quickly excuse myself from her presence and wander away wondering if I can just slip back upstairs into my room.

Being alone with my thoughts would beat being in this room full of phonies and wannabes.

Being dipped in a fiery pit headfirst would probably beat being down here.

# SIX

I'M near the steps, my getaway almost perfected when I hear my name being whispered.

"Over here," the voice says after I've twisted and turned, trying to find out who's calling me.

I see his head then, peeking from behind the sliding doors that lead into the small coatroom a few feet from the front door.

Antoine? What the hell? Is this the night for surprise visitors?

Crossing the floor quickly, I look around, hoping nobody sees me stepping into the coatroom, pushing Antoine back inside at the same time.

"So what happened the other night?"

His voice is still barely above a whisper, but it's just the way I remember it.

"What are you doing here?" I join him in whispering because the last thing I want is to have to try and explain why he's here on this night. Antoine is definitely not a member of Lincoln's elite and therefore not invited to this little party. Not that I think for one moment he'd be invited to anything else at this house, either—which is probably the biggest reason I don't want to like him.

There isn't a lot of room in the coatroom. Still, I try to

back up, to put some space between us. Antoine only closes that space, his eyes trained on mine as he does.

"Stop running, I'm not gonna hurt you."

His voice is a little lower, a tad sexier, and my heart does like a backward somersault in response. He's real close. I back up more, falling through some coats before my back hits the wall. He's right there, in my face, his hands flattening on the wall on both sides of my face.

I lick my lips. I do that a lot when I'm nervous. Either lick my lips or bite on the bottom one depending how edgy I'm feeling. Right now I probably could have bitten right through my lip, began bleeding to death and still not be able to move a muscle to get away from him.

"I'm...ah...I'm not running," I stammer. No way am I going to let him catch me speechless.

"You look real pretty in skirts, Sasha."

"Thank you, but you didn't answer my question."

"I'm here because you ran from me in the club the other night. And you run from me every day at school. I figured if I came to your house you wouldn't have anyplace else to run."

Logical, I think, but not wise. "Well, you picked a really bad time. My parents have company."

He nods. "So let's leave."

"I can't."

"Why not? You said your parents have company, not you."

He's got a pretty good point there. Besides, I've already had my fill of being nice, smiling and making small talk. Seeing Franklin's father was a shock, not to mention my mind's still trying to figure out what his research project is about. That I would discuss with Jake and Krystal at the library tomorrow. And the thought of having dinner with Alyssa sitting beside me complaining about Krystal and just about waging an all-out war against her is more than I want to deal with.

So why am I turning Antoine down this time?

Why can't I just slip out with him? He's already proven it's possible to sneak into this fortress my parents call a home. I should easily be able to slink out unnoticed.

"I can't," I say regardless.

"Can't or won't? What are you so afraid of, pretty girl?"

I'm not afraid of him. Or at least I don't think I am.

"I'm not afraid of anything."

"Then come on, let's go."

Before I can say another word, Antoine grabs my hand, opens the door and is leading us out into the foyer. I can hear the light music and conversation coming from the dining room. The only thing down this end is the front door and the coat closet. If anybody were to leave early they'd see us. Dinner hasn't even started yet so that's probably not an issue. Still, I walk a little faster.

We reach the door without a problem and slip out into the night air. It feels great against my skin. It was stuffy and crowded in the house with all those people. Antoine is still holding my hand. He's like a couple inches taller than me. I like that.

"I just wanted to see you." He starts talking the moment we clear the front steps and the stone path that lead down to the sidewalk in one direction then around to the back of the house in the other.

We're heading around back. There's a gazebo there just before you get to the swimming pool. I didn't think Antoine knew this because he's never been to my house before. Yet that's exactly where we go.

"Why do you keep saying I'm running from you?" I ask the minute we arrive at the gazebo. Antoine sits down on one of the two steps that lead you to the large center. I just keep standing in front of him.

"Because you are. Or at least you have been since the dance."

"That's not true."

"It is," he says seriously. "Look, you came to me asking all these questions about my brother who's been dead for months. Then when I try to talk to you about normal stuff you disappear. I kinda thought you might be feelin' me so I asked you out. You turned me down. *Running.* Then you show up at the club that I invited you to and disappear after the first dance. *Running* again."

"Wait a minute, I was at the club? At Trends?" He'd said that before, in the house, that I'd left him at the club.

I can't believe I actually just said that out loud. I mean, I'm thinking it of course. That night was a dream, that's what I decided. But he's saying it's true. I have to know if that's what he's saying for sure.

"Yeah."

"When?"

He looks like he thinks I might be losing my mind. Still, he shrugs and answers, "Friday night."

"Oh my god," I sigh. It was true. But how could I have been in my bed sleeping, with Mom and Casietta trying to wake me up, and at the club dancing with Antoine at the same time?

He reaches out, takes both my hands in his, pulling me until I'm standing between his outstretched legs.

"So I still think you're feelin' me but I don't know why you keep running from me. You're gonna have to just come right out and tell me. Do you like me or not?"

Oh please don't ask me that question. Please don't look at

me with those really dark brown eyes and wait for me to give you an answer. Please, please, please.

"Answer me, pretty girl."

"That's not my name," I say as a way to dodge his first question.

"But that's what you are."

Okay, my heart's not supposed to beat this fast. I'm almost positive it's not.

"It's not that I don't like you, Antoine." I figure this is the best answer I can give. Surely he's going to accept it.

"So if that's true, just say you *do* like me."

I should have known he'd be difficult. "Why?" I ask instead.

"Why do I want to hear you say it?"

"No." I shake my head. "Why do you like me?"

"That's easy," he says with a smile. "I like the way you look. The way you walk through the halls at school like you really want to be there. And I like that you're different from the other Richies."

"Different? How?" Because I really don't want to be like the rest of them. I just want to be me.

"You don't think you're better than anybody else," he answers simply.

Hmph, after tonight I'm not so sure that's true. I mean, hadn't I just stood in the room with a bunch of Richies talking about opening an exclusive club? If that doesn't say we're better than everybody else, I don't know what else does. But I don't tell Antoine that. He doesn't need to know.

Because I'm feeling comfortable with Antoine and the spring air is finally seasonal, with just a light breeze and temps over about sixty degrees, I sit quietly on the step just below him. He startles me by putting his fingers into my hair. I left it out tonight because that's what my mom instructed. Two crystal clips hold it back from my face.

"Your hair is soft," he says.

"Thanks."

It's quiet, but I want to say something. I want to keep talking to Antoine, to find out more about him. It's crazy, these weird feelings I have for him. One minute I don't want to see him and the next I can't see him soon enough.

Luckily, he seems to have all the answers. He's so sure about what he wants and who he wants it with, as if there are no obstacles or conflicts. I want to ask him about this but then I hear them.

The birds.

They're back.

Swarming around the top point of the gazebo they seem to just drop from the sky. The screeching is super loud and there are lots of them. More than I'd ever seen before. They swoop down first, yelling with some type of battle cry.

Antoine immediately bows over so that the top of his body is covering me. I feel the breeze of each bird whooshing by and know the only way I can escape them is to teleport as I have before when they attack. But I can't do that in front of Antoine. He'd think I'm some kind of freak, not a pretty girl.

The birds are flying lower, circling us, when Antoine yells, "Run to the house!"

Well, I'm not about to leave him out here with these birds that are out for something I'm sure he can't give them. They're connected to the Darkness. We all know they are. All of us except Antoine, of course. "No, you run. Get to your car."

I saw the old Hyundai looking sorely out of place amongst the BMWs, Mercedes and other expensive cars lined in our driveway when we came outside.

"C'mon, let's go!" he yells back, grabbing my hand.

We both stand and take off running, only to be stopped by Mouse's big body. By simply stretching out his arms, Mouse halts our escape. He's my bodyguard I guess because he's so big and so mean looking. How he got the name Mouse I have no idea. But my dad thought I needed somebody with me at all times, something about an important man like him having enemies. Maybe he owed somebody money, I don't know. But Mouse came with the great car, so I accepted him. Now I'm not convinced that was a wise decision.

Mouse looks at Antoine, then at me, and I don't know what scares me more at this moment—the birds or the look on Mouse's face. And just when I think he's going to grab us both by our collars and usher us into the house where we'd have to stand in front of the firing squad, i.e., my parents, Mouse does something totally confusing.

He grabs Antoine and starts walking him toward his car. Over his shoulder he shouts to me. "Disappear."

I'm standing there watching Mouse and Antoine's back when it dawns on me that the birds have vanished. I'm alone in the night.

Tossing Antoine into the driver's seat and slamming the door, Mouse turns to me one more time and gives me a curt nod.

I don't know why I did it. It's crazy and it's against the agreement I'd made with Krystal and with Jake. But somehow I know this is what Mouse means. He's telling me to disappear. And so I do.

# seven

To: princesssasha@lincolnmail.ing
From: wiccangoddess@cnettrix.ing
Re: Witch Trials

You are one of them. It's time we meet.

The message comes a little after midnight. I should be asleep, but my heart's still racing from the encounter at the gazebo. I half expect Mouse to come knocking on my door to question me. But he doesn't. As far as I know, Mouse never enters the house. He stays in a smaller house behind the pool. In the morning, he's at the car waiting for me. In the afternoon, he's at the school, at the car, waiting for me. Outside of that, I have no idea what he does with his time or where he goes when he's not with me. And up until a couple hours ago, I didn't really care. Funny how time changes things.

So Fatima wants to meet me. She says I'm one of them. One of who? I'd sent her the confusing message we found printed within the letter from Mary Burroughs and her response was that we meet. I want so badly to call Krystal and Jake, we need a powwow. I don't know how to respond to this woman. There are a few issues involved: 1) I only know this Fatima character from the internet; she could be some kind of psychopathic killer or something, for all I know; 2) what if she is legit and she's telling me that I'm one of them? Do I really want to know who "them" are? and 3) "them" could be a group of psychopathic killers who start out with freaky powers.

Okay, that's way more melodramatic than I intended. Anyway, I'm still trying to decide how to respond to Fatima when my cell phone rings. It's late, and I shouldn't be on the phone. But my parents are most likely passed out in their bedroom which is on the floor above mine, and Casietta is down the opposite end of the hall where her room is located. Odds are nobody hears the phone ringing but me, so I reach over to my nightstand and answer it.

"Who was that big guy? Your bodyguard?"

It's Antoine and I'm smiling already.

"Yeah, something like that."

"Man, dude is big. And he means business."

I can't believe he's calling me after what we'd just been through. I don't know that I'd be fast to call someone who was with me when we were attacked by birds. Then again, he has no clue that I'm probably what those birds were after.

"He's harmless. Never even raises his voice."

Antoine chuckles. "Yeah, I bet. So you're okay, right? I mean you didn't get into any trouble or anything for being out there with me?"

"No," I answer quickly. "Hey, wait a minute. How did you get my number?"

"Girl, you know I've got connections."

At his words, I wonder what those connections are. Friends at the cell phone store or friends who could not only dig up information on other people, but who could bury or literally dig up other people? Again with the melodramatics, I think I need a sedative or something. I don't know why I'm thinking of Antoine this way. Yeah, I do, because those are the types of unsavory things Antoine and his crew are known for.

"Well, you could have just asked me for it."

"I did and you said no."

"Then obviously, I didn't want you to have it."

"You did, you were just playing hard to get."

"And maybe I still am."

"Maybe you are. Anyway, I just wanted to make sure you were okay. See you in school tomorrow?"

He asks like he's not sure if I'm coming, which is weird because I rarely ever miss a day from school. There's absolutely nothing to do in this house all day long. School is usually the better option.

"I'll be in school."

"And you're not going to run from me again."

I'm starting to get a little irritated at his continued implication that I'm afraid of him. "I haven't been—"

"I know, you haven't been running," he says like he's getting tired of hearing me make that claim. Which we both know is a big fat lie. "So when I speak to you, you're gonna speak back?"

"It would be rude not to and I'm not rude."

Antoine laughs. "What if I want to sit with you at lunch?"

"I already have people to sit with."

"Okay, so do I. What if I wanted to walk you to your class?"

"Half my classes are GT, yours are on a different floor." That sounds exactly like I'm classifying us, and I immediately want to take it back.

But Antoine just chuckles and brushes it off, I guess. "And you say you're not playing hard to get. See you tomorrow, pretty girl."

Today's been weird. Everybody's talking about the missing tour bus. Word was the group had gone to some little town in

New Haven for a retreat. New Haven's not far from Lincoln. They'd come from Pennsylvania. A youth leader—I think somebody said his name was Minister Craig Hobbs—from this church where they actually have adults who pay attention to teenagers was in charge. Go figure. Along with Minister Hobbs were seven kids on the bus, three boys and four girls.

I wonder if their parents are worried. Lidia and Marvin probably wouldn't even notice if I vanished. That's a morbid thought, but I feel like it's really true. I didn't see either one of them this morning. Nor had they noticed that I ditched the party last night, ran out with a boy and was attacked by screeching birds. How could they not have noticed any of that? What kind of parents had a kid and then ignored them? The kind that, unfortunately, populate a good portion of the U.S.

So sad, but so true.

Anyway, it takes a lot of effort not to think about that missing bus of kids, especially since it's on everybody's mind. At lunch, Franklin joins us, so talking about what happened last night with Antoine and the birds is totally out of the question. He and Krystal cuddle most of the time. I eat my lunch, acting like their closeness isn't bothering me. But now I keep thinking about me and Antoine. Cuddling.

After school I head straight to my car and see Mouse standing by the driver's side door, waiting. He didn't let me drive this morning, and I'm almost positive he's not planning to let me drive now.

"I'm going to the library with a couple of friends. You know them—Jake and Krystal. They should be coming along soon."

Mouse just nods, but he's watching me in a weird way. Well, weirder than he normally does. I notice that he's wearing all black. I think he always wears that color ensemble. Every day, black pants, black shoes, black shirt, black jacket. He could be related to Faith Hughes, the Goth girl who sits by the soda machine in the cafeteria. Except Mouse doesn't have all the piercings. What he does have is a lot of muscles, like I just really noticed that today. His arms are like cannons and his neck is thick and short like a football player's. His face is kind of rugged, his skin the color of mud. But he doesn't look mean or scary, just strange and maybe intimidating. I guess that's his purpose as my bodyguard.

"You ready to go?" Jake approaches, but I barely hear him, I'm so busy staring at Mouse.

"Where's Krystal?"

Jake shrugs, long locks of brown hair scraping over his forehead. His backpack is on his right shoulder, and his hands are stuffed into the pockets of his hoodie, just like always.

I've known Jake since I was a kid. Since we were both kids. We kind of hooked up because we had something in common. I could disappear, and he could lift things like cars or trucks or anything else no normal human should be able to lift. The moment we found out we were both freaks, we became instant friends.

Now there's Krystal, her appearance in Lincoln invading our little twosome. Me, I was thrilled to see there was someone else with the mark Jake and I shared because that meant she must have powers like us, too. And she did.

Jake, I can't really tell how he feels about Krystal moving to Lincoln. Sometimes I think he really likes her and wishes Krystal could see that. Then other times, like now, I don't know. He looks like he'd rather eat one of those maniacal birds that keep following us than wait another second for Krystal.

"We have to wait," I say and look away from him because I don't want to see his reaction. It's not going to change my mind either way. "I've got something to tell you two."

"You can tell me," he says and sounds irritated.

"We're all in this together. I'm telling both of you."

I do look at him then, but he just sighs and opens the car door. It's a two-door, so I watch absently as he pushes the front seat up and climbs in the back. With Mouse driving, it probably makes sense for me to ride in the back today and let Krystal ride shotgun.

Fifteen minutes later, we climb out of the car and walk up the steps to the library. Jake is quiet, but Krystal's talking about how she really enjoyed the Bible study she went to with her mother last night. I'm only half listening to her because there's so much more on my mind.

We go all the way to the back of the library because there are a lot of other kids there, and we don't want to be disturbed. But Jake stops in the mythology section first and picks up some books. Krystal changes her line of conversation the minute he's out of earshot.

"So listen to this, Franklin asked me about doing it."

I drop my bag down onto the table. It makes a loud thunking noise that has a couple of kids looking up from the table two rows over. Rolling my eyes at them, I return my gaze to Krystal and just stare. *"It?"*

She nods with a smile that doesn't quite look happy. "Yeah, *it.*"

"Like he wants to do it, with you?"

She nods again.

Wow. Sex. Hmm.

"So what did you tell him?"

"Nothing really, just kind of brushed it off."

"Well, do you want to? With him, you know, do you want to have sex with him?"

She sits down and drums her fingers on the table. Krystal

doesn't have nails, so the sound is dull, monotonous. "I don't know."

Krystal's a pretty girl, with her creamy coffee-toned skin and high cheekbones. I guess this is why Franklin is cuddling so much with her. He obviously wants to go to the next step. I wonder what she'll do and figure since I'm her friend, I should like offer some advice. Problem is I don't really have any as I'm still holding tight to my virginity as well.

"You should think about it, don't do anything you're not totally comfortable with."

She nods her head. "Yeah, that's what I was thinking."

Jake returns.

"They've got a whole section on mythology—Roman, Indian, Celtic, Greek. I just grabbed a bunch. So let's just look through them all and find any references to the River Styx." Jake is talking and giving out books to me and Krystal like Mr. Emory, the science teacher.

We all sit down and I speak up first. "Before we look through the books, I have to tell you guys something."

"Okay, shoot," Jake says but opens up his book like he's going to read while I talk.

Very rude, but I don't bother to say anything since he's obviously in a funk. Besides, once I start talking, I'm sure he'll give me his undivided attention.

"I saw the birds last night," I begin and wait for their reactions.

"Oh," Krystal says. "We haven't seen them since before the blizzard. What happened?"

After going over this back and forth and debating whether or not I should leave out the fact that I was with Antoine when the birds attacked, I decide to just tell it all. I have no idea if Antoine had told his clique about what happened, so it's logical that I just tell mine the truth.

"I was out at the gazebo talking to Antoine and they just attacked."

As predicted, Jake stops turning pages in the book and looks up at me. "Wait, last night? I thought you had some party to go to."

"I did, but then Antoine showed up and—"

"Antoine, as in Antoine Watson?" Krystal's raised brow means she has a lot more questions. "He was invited to the party and we weren't?"

Now, that wasn't exactly the line of questioning I thought she'd take. "No. Of course he wasn't invited. He just sort of showed up."

"At your house?"

That was Jake asking suspiciously. "Yeah, at my house." Okay, why are they latching on to the Antoine thing more than the birds? "You guys, I said those birds are back and they attacked me. Don't you think that's cause for alarm?"

Krystal smiles. "I think what we really need to know is how Antoine found out where you lived and since when did he just start dropping by?"

I sigh because I guess I'm going to have to get this part over with. This part being the new boy interrogation. "Okay, abbreviated version—ever since I talked to him about Ricky he's been trying to get with me. I've been ignoring him but obviously he hasn't gotten the message. Now can we get back to the serious business?"

"Seems to me you don't really want him to get a message if you're talking to him at the gazebo." This is Jake who looks back down at his book the minute his words are out.

Okay, let's try another tactic. "I think I have a new power," I blurt out and have the pleasure of watching both of them look at each other, then immediately at me, like I just grew a new head.

"What is it?"

I shrug. "Don't really know. All I know is that one minute I was lying in my bed thinking about…" I hesitate before saying his name again. "I was thinking about stuff and then the next thing you know I'm across town at Trends dancing the night away."

"You teleported all the way across town?" Jake talks slowly, like I was speaking another language.

I'm already shaking my head. "No. I don't think it's the same as teleporting. My body was still in my room and there was another me at the club."

"Another you? How is that possible?" Krystal asks.

"Don't know. Was hoping you guys could tell me."

Krystal drums her fingers on the table again. This little action is going to get annoying. Quick.

She doesn't seem to notice the way I look down at her hands then back up at her, mentally willing her to stop. Guess that's because neither me nor her have mind-reading capabilities. "So your powers are manifesting, too. And the birds are back. The Darkness will follow."

"And we still don't know what it is or what it wants," Jake adds.

"There's more," I say, pulling Mary Burroughs's letter out of my bag in the envelope that I put it in last night so it wouldn't tear. I give it to Jake. "I sent Fatima what was written on the letter. Her response was this—you are one of them. It's time we meet."

"Fatima, the witch?" Krystal asks.

"Practicing witch," Jake amends. "There's no such thing as real witches."

Me and Krystal stare at him.

"But there is such a thing as Mystyx and superpowers?" Krystal says.

"You know what I mean," Jake rebuts. "We're here because of energy surges in the weather. What would be the explanation for witches? Why are they here? How did they come to be?"

"Hmm, this is really bothering you. This not knowing or not being able to rationalize," another voice interjects.

Just like she always seems to do, Lindsey simply walks up to our table and starts talking. Yet this time, like yesterday, her words are right on point. She's looking at Jake as if she can see through him. Through her thin bangs, I see that her forehead is scrunched.

"You want to know all the answers now. They're coming too slow." She keeps talking and keeps looking at Jake.

"Shut up and go away," he says, frowning and looking back down to his book.

"Ah, really, Lindsey, this is kind of a private conversation," Krystal interjects.

Lindsey turns to look at Krystal. Her hair is pulled into a ponytail today, one that swishes behind her as she moves. "You guys have a lot of private conversations. I've noticed that about you."

"Okay, that's fine. Now can you leave us to our private conversation?" Krystal rolls her eyes, something that seems uncharacteristic for her.

"It's okay if you're still on the fence about Franklin. Sex is a big step. You should actually wait until you're married but statistics say that by the age of fifteen approximately thirteen percent of teenage girls have had intercourse. So I guess you could say you're ready. Statistically, I mean."

I think Krystal's jaw will break, her mouth opens so wide. Then again, mine opens just as fast and probably just as wide. How did she know what Krystal and I had just talked about?

"What?" Krystal clears her throat. "I don't know what you're talking about."

Lindsey pulls up a chair from the table across from us and puts her book bag down on the floor. For a minute she just stares at us, then she lifts her leg—and because she's wearing a jean skirt with pink ruffle at the bottom—we can immediately see her left ankle.

"So am I officially a member of the club now?" she asks, sitting back and crossing her arms. Her smile is smug, but her eyes still look like she's seeking permission.

"Oh…my…" Krystal can't even finish she's so shocked by what she sees.

Jake grabs Lindsey's ankle and just about yanks her across the table. "Where'd you get that? Did you paint that on?" he's asking, but he's already rubbing her skin fiercely, and it's not coming off.

"No. Let go of me!" Lindsey protests, pushing Jake's hands away. "I was born with it. Just as I suspect you guys were. I saw Krystal's at the dance and thought it was just a coincidence. Then when we were in gym changing our clothes I saw yours, Sasha."

She looks over at Jake with unmasked agitation. "You're always covered from head to toe, so I don't know where yours is, but I'll bet my next year's allowance you've got one."

All I can do is nod. Yes, Jake has one. Just like me and Krystal and now Lindsey. We all have the same *M* birthmark.

# eight

which means we all have powers.

Lindsey's I'm betting has something to do with mind reading.

"How long have you been able to do that?" I ask because my other two cohorts still look like something's swallowed their tongues.

Lindsey looks at me, her brown eyes settling on mine. She huffs, and her wispy bangs lift and fall on her forehead. "Seems like forever. But I think it really hit me that I was different when I was around twelve."

"How does it work?"

"I'm telepathic. If I look at you I can hear your thoughts."

Krystal rebounds next. "At any time you can read my thoughts? Or anybody else's thoughts?"

Lindsey shrugs. "Sort of. I mean, over the years I've figured out what keeps a lot of thoughts from crowding me."

I'm curious, so I ask, "And what's that?"

"The color black."

"Huh?" Jake looks like he's about to bolt at any second.

"If the person's wearing black or I'm wearing black, I can't get a read on their thoughts. So when I'm in a mood or just want the thoughts to shut up, I wear black." She shrugs. "I mean, I could just not look at people and their thoughts would stay in their heads, but how long can I do that and lead a normal, productive social life? Know what I mean?"

"So why the color black?"

"Don't know. Never figured that out. I was just so relieved to find something that worked. I just go with the flow."

"Really? So you're saying all you have to do is look at me and you can tell exactly what I'm thinking?"

At his doubting question, Lindsey turns, looks directly at Jake and says, "She's more open to it than you think. Just tell her you like her and get it over with."

Jake's cheeks turn a shade of pink I've never seen on a boy before. Guessing who the "she" is in Lindsey's assessment of Jake's mind was a no-brainer. Although I doubt Krystal has figured that out yet. I can't help it. I chuckle.

"Not. Funny." Jake shifts in his chair and flips open another book. "I'm wearing black from now on," he mumbles.

"Welcome to the Mystyx," Krystal says, extending her hand across the table to Lindsey. "If you could just keep my thoughts in your head, that would be real cool."

Lindsey smiles, taking Krystal's offered hand. "I know how to respect people's privacy. To the extent that's possible for someone like me."

I'm just about to answer her when I get a familiar sensation in the pit of my stomach. It's like millions of tiny stars are moving inside of me, lifting me until I'm floating.

And then it's black again, the total darkness that I've seen before. I feel weightless but not necessarily afraid this time. I'm going someplace. I can hear my name being called and it feels like someone is pulling me along, taking me to where they want me to be.

"Sasha," the gentle voice is saying once more.

It's closer now. This person, this woman, is closer to me.

The darkness seems just a little lighter this time (if that's possible) or maybe just the spot where I stare because I think that's where the voice is coming from. I don't know, but my heart's pounding so hard I feel like screaming with its rapid pace.

"Stay calm," the voice says. "You're still in control."

"In control of what?" I ask the absolute nothingness that's there since it's obviously talking to me.

I mean really, behind me there's this dark place that I remember going through before I showed up at the nightclub with Antoine. And in front of me there's all this light, like a bunch of combined headlights shining directly my way.

"She said you would come, you and your friends."

"Who said that?"

"It doesn't matter now. I've been sent to give you this message. Be vigilant, all of you. He's coming back and this time he threatens everything."

"Who? What are you talking about?" The light is dimming, my eyes stop blinking so fiercely at its brightness.

"The light will prevail," the voice says slowly. "The light always prevails."

The ending words are a whisper just as the last flickers of light are sucked away. A cool wind blows around me, and before I can open my mouth to ask another question—which would most likely go unanswered like my previous ones—I feel that floating sensation again.

Floating, but faster. More like falling this time.

Falling and falling until I feel the cool tile of the library floor and hear the loud thunk of the chair I was sitting in hitting the floor beside me.

"Sasha? Sasha?"

I come through this time to Krystal cradling my head in her lap and Lindsey holding my hand and plucking my cheeks at the same time. I can't see Jake, but I know he's there. They're all calling my name.

"Shh," is the first thing I manage to say. "We're in the library, remember."

"You should think about that before you go dozing off and falling out of your chair."

See, I knew Jake was here.

"I didn't fall asleep," I say, rubbing my eyes and struggling to sit up.

"Then what happened?" Lindsey asks. "First you were talking and then you weren't and then you fell."

I pull my hand out of her grip because I don't know if her mind-reading abilities increase with contact. She pulls the other hand from my cheek, which probably has a huge red mark on it by now from all her pinching.

"It was that thing again. The manifestation of my powers. I went to the same place." Then I think about what I am saying. "It was the same but different."

By this time Krystal is helping me up off the floor and we're all taking our seats again. Me, after Jake had picked up my chair.

"So you, like, black out or something?" Krystal asks when we're all at the table.

She's sitting to my right and Lindsey's to my left. Jake's across from us, his forehead scrunched up like he's a fuse waiting to blow. I think he has anger management issues and, considering how strong he is, know that this can become a real problem.

"No. I'm awake. At least wherever it is that I go I'm awake."

Jake's shaking his head negatively. "You definitely looked asleep just before you slid out of the chair."

"That's what my mom and Casietta said when they were standing over my bed the last time. They said they'd been trying to wake me up. But I wasn't asleep, I just wasn't there."

"It's called astral projection," Lindsey volunteers, nodding her head as if she'd just figured everything out.

"What?" I ask.

"How do you know?" Jake says through clenched teeth.

Lindsey looks over at him, then reaches across the table and touches his hand. "There's nothing to be afraid of, Jake. It's a part of her powers. Like she said, they're growing." Turning her attention from Jake back to me, she continues, "Astral projection is where your astral body travels to another plane. But your physical body stays in one place."

Out of the corner of my eye I can see Krystal shaking her head. "How do you know all this?"

Lindsey shrugs. "I have a lot of time to myself so I read different things. It sticks. Kind of like a photographic memory."

Jake sits back in his chair, folding his arms over his chest. "Mind reading and photographic memory, I guess those are your powers."

He's skeptical of Lindsey, has been since day one. Problem is, he can't argue with the swirling *M* on her ankle.

"Nah, I think the memory thing is just natural," Lindsey says, then kind of looks past Jake.

For a few seconds she's quiet, and I almost think *she's* astral projected somewhere.

"So okay, my power is manifesting and I'm traveling to some other plane and then reappearing in different places. How is that a power I can use? The voice said we had to be vigilant, that he was coming back for everything this time."

"Who?" Jake questions.

Krystal simultaneously asks, "What voice?"

"The one I saw when I astral floated or whatever she called it. She said that we were to be vigilant, all of us. And that he was coming for everything this time. She also said that the light always prevails."

"The light prevails. The light prevails," Lindsey repeats. "I've heard that saying somewhere."

"Did she say anything about the River Styx?" Jake asks, pulling one of the books from the pile he'd been reading. "I really think that's a connection."

"I do, too," Krystal chimes in.

"I want to know what those birds have to do with anything," I say.

"They're probably watching us," Lindsey says.

"What?" All three of us—me, Jake and Krystal ask in unison.

"You know, like a spy of sorts. In the movies there's always warlocks or sorcerers and they send their familiars to go and search out their prey. Like the black cat skulking about. That's usually a witch's familiar. Birds can be familiars, too. The Greeks loved using winged creatures," Lindsey answers as if everything she just said was common knowledge. I guess the girl must have had a lot of free time to read stuff.

"It's closing time." The librarian, with her tight curly hair and chocolate-brown leatherlike skin, comes over and taps on the table.

Glancing at my watch, I see it's seven fifty-seven. The library closes at eight. We've been here for over three hours. It didn't seem like that long.

"Why don't we do this." Lindsey starts talking again. With her elbows on the table she leans forward, whispering to us. "Sasha and I will look into the thing about the birds and the email from Fatima."

I told Krystal and Jake about this before Lindsey showed up, but then again, if she could read minds, she really didn't need me to actually say it.

"You and Krystal start working on the river connection," she keeps right on talking.

Krystal is standing, grabbing her purse and shaking her head. "That sounds good."

"Yeah, great," Jake says, standing up but not looking at Krystal.

"We'll meet up again Friday after school," I add.

"Oh, we've got that science trip Friday afternoon to the Nature Center. Are you guys going?" Krystal asks.

"I don't have earth science," Lindsey says. "I'm taking the GT biology and science fair preparation."

"Lucky you," Jake says. "I'm going on the trip."

"Mrs. Paul asked me to go as a sort of chaperone so I can earn some of my service hours," I say.

"You're the same age as us. How are you chaperoning?" Krystal asks me, looking like she doesn't believe a word I've just said.

"Because I've taken the earth science class and aced it, she thinks I can go to answer any questions or whatever. It's no big deal."

"Yup, no big deal. It's so easy for some of us," Jake says and walks away.

"Okay, so what is up with his funky attitude?" Lindsey asks.

"Can't you just read his mind and tell?" I ask.

"No. It doesn't work like that. I get snatches of thoughts but sometimes they don't all go together."

Krystal just shrugs and starts walking toward the entrance. "He's just upset about his grades. Wants to make sure he keeps up his GPA so he can get into college."

"That's crazy. Jake's smart, of course he'll get in."

We're at the door. Jake had already gone through and Krystal was now pushing the revolving glass and brass door. Lindsey is between us and I'm holding up the rear. Outside is cool and we all migrate toward Mouse and the car.

"It's not just about getting in, Sasha. He has to get almost perfect grades to get a full scholarship. He can't afford to go to college otherwise."

I know this, or at least I know that it's Jake's goal to go to college and get out of Lincoln. I also know that his father, who works as a janitor at the local electric company, doesn't make a lot of money, and most of it goes to the part-time private nurse hired to take care of Jake's grandfather.

"He'll get in and he'll be able to go," I say confidently.

Jake is my friend, and like I said he's smart. If anybody deserves to go to college, make something of himself and get out of this boring small town, it's him. So I'm declaring he'll go to college, if I have to dip into my trust fund to pay for it.

After all, we're more than just friends. All four of us are so much more.

And as I walk thinking these thoughts, I happen to look up, and strange as it seems, there's the moon. Well, half the moon, but it's already sitting quietly in the sky as if it belongs there at this time. It's spring, almost summer, days are already longer, so it's still semi-light outside. As a matter of fact, if I turn and look the other way, I can still see the fading orb that is the sun. Both of them are in the sky tonight, sharing space and yet keeping their distance.

Clouds shift, and just before climbing into the car, I swear they form a letter, an *M* swirling on masses of billowy puffiness.

We, now the four of us, are definitely more than friends. We're the ones who need to be vigilant. The ones I suspect are supposed to stop whoever "he" is and the "everything" he's coming back for.

Question is, how are we going to do that?

# nine

TONY is a Jet. That's a member of a group of white Americans who believe they are the "true" Americans.

Maria's brother, Bernardo, is a Shark. The Sharks are first generation Americans from Puerto Rico.

The Jets and the Sharks don't like each other.

But Tony likes Maria. And Maria likes Tony.

And that's a problem.

Man, can I relate to this. Sitting in Mrs. Copaceptic's English II Honors class is more uncomfortable today than any of the days yet this year. Last year we read William Shakespeare's *Romeo and Juliet* and watched the movie with Claire Danes and Leonardo DiCaprio. This year Mrs. Copaceptic—for reasons I'll never understand—wanted to pick up on the same theme of star-crossed lovers, I suppose. We're watching *West Side Story*, the 1950s musical that's a remake of the way outdated *Romeo and Juliet*.

I guess this is outdated too since it's over fifty years ago. Still, I think I like this version better. Maybe it's because I'm multicultural with my dad being what they'd call "white American" and my mom being Argentinean. I suppose I'd be considered a member of the Sharks.

But then what would that make Antoine?

He's definitely not "white American." African-American,

yes. So he'd be a twenty-first century Jet. We'd be the new generation Tony and Maria.

If I wasn't so undecided about being with him.

The thing is, it's not all about the racial issue for me. My reason for hesitating where Antoine's concerned is more about my parents. About what their reaction would be to me bringing Antoine over for dinner or even taking him to prom. Dad would flip and Mom would spazz for a couple of hours, then give me some long boring speech about my responsibilities, my duties to my father, my family. Which is all a bunch of bull, but she's been brainwashed to believe it.

Casietta says it's because back home in Buenos Aires, my mother had nothing. My father was literally her knight in shining armor, rescuing her from poverty and hunger. You'd think that would make her more sympathetic to others less fortunate, instead of more judgmental. In return for my father's rescue, she worships him, making every word that comes out of his mouth—and some that don't—like a newly revised bible.

Sighing, because that's all I can do when I think about my home situation, I slouch in my chair. My chin's leaning on my arm as I watch Maria singing on half the screen and Tony on the other.

They're so in love.

My cell phone vibrates in my purse, so using very slow motions so as not to tip Mrs. Copaceptic off that I'm alive, I pull it free and look at it.

Thinking about u

The text from Antoine makes me blush. So with one hand attempting to cover the lower half of my face that's heated and smiling, I answer with the other.

Thinking about u 2

A few seconds later...

Meet me n hall B after class

My heart's thumping. Hallway B is on the other side of the building. It leads to the music room and the culinary classes. But those classes are only open Monday through Wednesday.

Ok

Suddenly I can't wait until Bernardo finds out about Tony and Maria. I can't wait until the big hand circles past three more numbers on the clock and the bell rings. In essence, I'm ready to go.

Time works in my favor because before I can drift into another musical scene, the bell sounds. I gather my stuff up quickly and move through the rush of twenty or so kids trying to get as far away from English as they possibly can for the next few hours, until we're forced to endure it all again tomorrow.

Moving through the halls, I'm ignoring everybody else around me, all the while hoping I look okay. I have on a yellow jersey dress with thin white leggings with yellow print and my white leather Mary Janes. My hair's pulled up in the front with a white clip, hanging down in the back. With my free hand I reach back and sort of fluff it up. My heart's beating wildly as the direction I'm walking kind of empties of students because nobody really belongs down this part of the school at this time.

With a flattened palm, I push through the double doors and take the first few steps into hallway B, only to be grabbed at the waist and pulled to the side against a bank of lockers.

"Hey, pretty girl," he says in that not-too-deep-but-still-sexy voice.

My toes curl, and I almost lose my grip on my books. "Hey," I say in what I think is a light and airy tone.

Then there are no more words. Antoine's lips are on mine

and I'm sinking. Not floating or flying or soaring, but sinking. Falling deeper and deeper into the touch of his lips on mine, the scent of his cologne so close to me. His arms wrap around me, his hands opening flat on my back. I'm still holding my books, so my fingers grip them tighter between us. He tilts his head, and I feel his tongue brush over my bottom lip.

Tiny tingles move throughout my body like a swarm of bees. His one hand is on my back, but the other soon starts to move lower and lower, until I think my dress is coming up. Now my heart feels like it's running a marathon, and my body's trying to catch up. I start shaking my head because the kiss is getting deeper and the once soft touch of Antoine's hands is now a little harder.

My fingers loosen a bit on my books, and I'm able to maneuver my free hand to flatten on Antoine's chest. For a moment I pause because, hey, his heart's beating just as fast as mine. So anyway, I can analyze that later. I push against his chest and try to close my mouth. He's reluctant and is still pushing his lips on mine. But I turn my head so now he's not getting lip, but cheek. Finally he pulls back and looks at me.

It's a strange kind of look, like he's confused and flustered all at the same time. I slip away from him and lean over to put my books down on the floor. When I rise, I smooth back my hair and take a deep breath.

"Is that what you were thinking about when you texted me?" I'm trying to calm my breathing down. Trying to wrap my mind around that heated kiss and the feel of Antoine's hand on my butt.

Antoine backs up and leans against the locker. He's wearing dark-colored jeans, with the fronts sort of washed out. They're long and baggy but not hanging under his tennis shoes like some of the other guys. His shirt is button-down and lifts at the sides when he tries to push his hands into his pants pockets. For a second I just look at his face. It's the complexion of chocolate—milk, not dark. He has a thin mustache trying to come in and slightly thick lips. Lips that I remember intimately. Okay, blushing again. So not cool.

I look away.

"I was just thinking about you," he finally answers.

I nod my head like I understand, but I don't.

"I'm not like that, you know." He doesn't say anything, just stares at me. "I mean, I don't just let guys kiss and touch all over me in hallways. That's not what I do."

He nods his head. "I know."

"Then what is this?"

He shrugs. "I just wanted to see you and when I did, guess I just got carried away."

We've really got the nodding part of our relationship down to a science because I nod again, too. Funny thing is, I think I got carried right away with him.

"So we should get to class."

"Can I get a hug?" he asks, but he doesn't move.

I'm skeptical. Didn't we just hug? Well, not actually. His arms were around me, but mine weren't on him. But if I hug him we might kiss again. And if we kiss again...

"Just a hug, Sasha. I get what you said about us being in school and all. So I'm just asking for a hug."

I'm hesitant, and then I'm not because I know I want to hug him. And yeah, I probably want to kiss him, too. Hormones are a bi-atch!

So I walk over and stand in front of him. He still hasn't taken his hands out of his pockets.

"We shouldn't," I say because suddenly, being this close to him means something different. Something I hadn't thought of before rushing to meet him in this secluded space.

"Why not?" He stands up straight and takes his hands out of his pockets. "Other people do it."

"But we're not them."

"I know," he says, and his voice is lowering as his hands are lifting to touch both sides of my face. "We're better than the others. That's why we'll last."

His touch is soft, and I take a step closer, feeling the temperature around me change.

"Is that what you want? For us to last?"

He nods, whispers "yes," then kisses my lips lightly. No tongue this time, just lips, and it's as sweet as it was the first time. And surprisingly, still as unsettling.

We are just pulling away from each other, like in slow motion. Our lips and bodies no longer touching, but Antoine's hands are still on my shoulders and mine are just barely moving away from his waist when we hear the sound.

Heels click on the floor, growing closer.

"Well. Well. Well. Isn't this…interesting."

The voice is laced with sarcasm. If it were an adult, a teacher, the principal, I would feel ten times better than I do right now.

Jumping away from Antoine like he's a walking flame, I turn to see Alyssa standing not three feet away from us. What is she doing in hallway B, and why on earth did she pick this moment to be cruising by?

"Hey, Alyssa." I'm trying to sound all nonchalant while I bend over and get my books.

"Sasha," she says without even looking at me. Her eyes are glued to Antoine. And when I look over at him, he's frowning because it's no secret around school that Alyssa's a bitch.

"Slumming, I see," she follows up, taking a step closer to Antoine. "Shouldn't you be downstairs in one of your remedial classes?" Then, before he can answer, she puts up a finger and says, "Oh, no. I forgot, maybe you should be out robbing someone or trying to sell some drugs."

My stomach twists and I feel my cheeks burning. Antoine's frown deepens, but he stands right up to her. "If I wanted drugs I could just get them from your brother. No need to go outside the school for that."

I swallow the giggle that threatens to erupt. Antoine is right. Rumor is that Alyssa's older brother Ronald sells drugs. Supposedly, he gets them from some guy in New York and sells them here. Lincoln isn't known for having a lot of crime or drug-related activity, possibly because there's not many people here. Still, they say Ronald has a pretty good clientele. But Ronald graduated last year. I don't know what he's doing now.

Alyssa's lips press into a tight line. "Don't overstep your boundaries just because she's unwisely giving you attention." And when she said "she," her head jerked in my direction.

"As for you, I really don't think this is what your parents had in mind when they asked us to get all the kids on board with the new project."

I hate that she's right. Hate that her words and her anger are just confirming what I figured would happen if Antoine and I were publicly dating.

"It's not like that," I say and know it sounds lame.

"Yeah, right," she says. "Come on or we're going to be late."

She starts walking, and I know she's expecting me to follow her. I really don't want to, and I look at Antoine who's just about spewing smoke from his ears, he's so mad. I take a step in the direction Alyssa went, and he reaches out, grabbing my arm.

"I can walk you," he says.

"Sasha." Alyssa's voice echoes through the hallway as she tosses me a look over her shoulder. "Are you coming?"

For a minute I feel like the proverbial deer caught in head-lights. I look from one of them to the other with wide eyes and can't seem to make up my mind. Then I, as gently as I can under the circumstances, pull out of Antoine's grasp and whisper, "I've gotta go."

His arm falls to his side, and I know he's pissed at me. I hurry up and walk away. Alyssa stays a few steps ahead of me, and I don't try to catch up with her. Because for as much as I concede that she's right, I don't want to be walking down the hall with her any more than I'd wanted to leave Antoine standing there.

# ten

It's a little after eleven. I should be asleep, but I'm not. I can't, just like I couldn't concentrate the rest of the day at school, and I couldn't wait to finish with dinner so I could come to my room to be alone.

Alone to think about what happened with Antoine in hallway B.

I'd be lying if I didn't admit I enjoyed every second of our time together. But at the same time, it would also be a lie to say I hadn't been thinking that it was wrong the entire time.

Dropping an arm over my forehead, I sigh because really, life should not be this hard. Why can't I just be a normal teenager, go to school dances, have crushes, eat cheeseburgers? I mean really, why does my entire life have to be filled with conflict and indecision? There's not one thing I can do in life without wondering who it will effect or how it will effect them. It's such a rip-off!

Antoine enters my mind again. Not that he ever leaves it for very long these days. He said he'd been thinking about me. I wonder if he is right now. I wonder what he's doing and who he's doing it with. I should call him. No, it's too late.

But I sort of miss him. I want to hear his voice. Rolling over, I grab my cell phone from the nightstand and text him.

Sorry about 2day
Thinking of u

Then I wait.

And wait.

Like a half hour goes by and there's no response from him. He's really mad at me. Is it over? Or is this like our first boyfriend/girlfriend spat? Are we boyfriend and girlfriend?

Questions roll throughout my mind like I'm a contestant on *Are You Smarter Than A Fifth Grader?* And since I have none of the answers, it's apparent that I'm not.

What should I do now?

Rolling over to my side I fake fluff my pillows and curl up. Maybe I should just go to sleep. Can't.

I need to see him.

Need to talk to him. To explain.

And just like that I'm on the move again.

This time I know the cool darkness I'm floating through is another plane—an astral plane, as Lindsey says. So I'm not afraid or confused. In fact, this time I know exactly where I'm going.

When I open my eyes the room I'm in is dark, lit only by the moon. It's the first quarter moon, day seven of the moon's life cycle, when there's ninety degrees between the moon, the sun and the earth. For a few seconds, I simply stare at it. The silvery gray half sphere sitting silently in the abyss of black. Light in the dark, I sometimes think of it.

Then my gaze roams around the rest of the room. It's small, less than half the size of mine. Actually, it's more like the size of my closet. Behind me is a dresser with a small TV on one end and a bunch of tubes and containers on the other. In front of me is a bed, twin-size. And lying on the bed is Antoine.

My heart thuds at the sight, and I take a step closer to the bed. I'm in his bedroom, it dawns on me suddenly. Thinking about him, feeling the urgent need to be with him, has brought me here. This is crazy, this new power of mine. It's surreal how I can be in one place and in another at the same time. Taking soft steps, I move around the bed until I'm standing at the top of the bed near Antoine's head.

He only has one pillow, whereas I have four on my bed, not counting the decorative ones Casietta insists on adding. I don't know why I keep making these comparisons between me and Antoine, what I have and what he has or doesn't have. Habit, I guess. The one thing, I'm slowly realizing, he's definitely got a grip on is my heart.

It's thudding faster now as I reach out a hand and lightly touch his cheek. Surprisingly, it's kind of soft. I wouldn't, under other circumstances, classify a boy's skin as soft, but it is. The bottom half of him is beneath a sheet, but his shoulder and his arm are bare. I touch there, too, letting just the tips of my fingers feel his skin.

It grows deeper, this feeling I have for him swirling inside me. So deep I just want to jump inside, to leave everything else behind and just be...with him.

In the distance I hear my name being called and I jump. Looking around, I make sure I'm the only one in this room, the only one who isn't supposed to be in this room. Antoine doesn't stir. He probably doesn't hear the voice. My time is running out. I know this because I can hear the voice and not see the person behind it. I'm going to astral project back to my room soon, so I lean forward until I'm just inches away from Antoine's face. His breath is warm against my skin, and I close my eyes to the comfort. Getting a little closer, I kiss his cheek. Once. Twice. On the third time it feels like I'm kissing the air.

I'm already traveling through the plane, moving on my way back to my room. It's all good because I was able to see Antoine, to touch him and be near him. I should be able to sleep now.

Then I hear my name again.

"Sasha Carrington. You are one of them."

So at first I thought there was nothing else to fear in this dark place but now I'm thinking again. I feel like I've stopped moving, like the transition from one place to another has been halted.

"You are wrong."

Who is this talking to me? I look around and expect to see the circle of light I saw before, even though the voice I hear this time is deep and raspy, not high-pitched and sing-songy like the one before. But I don't see any light, none at all.

"Who are you?" I ask, knowing instinctively that I won't get an answer.

Then I think I see something swirling in the distance, like smoke, building from wisps on the floor to a dark funnel that grows closer. Wind blows all around me, strong and so cool that chill bumps prick my skin. My hair's flying around my face, tendrils going into my eyes and touching my lips. Then it stops, the funnel of dark smoke and the wind. I blink and blink again, trying to focus. All I see is more darkness but this time in the shape of a huge man.

Like over seven feet as-wide-as-a-doorway kind of man. There is no face, but the voice talks again.

"Come with me. Help me."

"I don't know who…or what you are," I say, hoping this will serve as an answer.

"I am all. I will be all. Help me and you will be spared."

"Spared from what?"

The form comes closer, leaning down so that what I presume is its head is right next to my ear.

"Death," it whispers.

Chills run from my eardrum down my spine to wrap around my ankles like shackles, and I scream.

I come through on my bed, kicking and flailing my arms, in an attempt to get away from that thing. Finally realizing that I'm back at home in my room by myself, I calm down a little. My heart still beats too fast, but I open my eyes now, staring up at my ceiling, remembering when there were stars painted there. The absence of my stars makes me think of the moon, and I turn to my side, look out my bedroom window and find what I'm searching for.

The moon.

My moon.

Going through its normal cycle, yet reminding me of something. Trying to remind me of something that I should know. I keep staring at it, seeing the craters and murky gray aura that circles it.

"What are you saying? What are you trying to tell me?" I ask in a whisper, hoping desperately that whatever it is I'll find out before that thing kills me and everybody else.

*The oldest and strongest emotion of mankind is fear.*
—H.P. Lovecraft

# eleven

This has got to be the most boring field trip I've ever attended. And since it's the first I've attended as a student/chaperone, it's even worse.

Antoine is walking next to me, with Jake, Krystal and Franklin behind me. I know they're wondering what's going on with me and Antoine, but they don't ask, so I don't volunteer any info.

This trip is taking way too long. We were inside the Nature Center for the first half, about three hours. That was a little better because at least it was air-conditioned inside the redbrick building located just beyond the south end of the lake. Lunch was in the Nature Center's eatery, if you could really call it that. Ten round tables with hard blue chairs on midnight blue linoleum with sparkles that made it look like the night sky. There was a snack bar with soft pretzels, cold cardboard pizza slices and watered-down fruit punch. But mostly everybody had bought their own lunch.

Antoine hadn't. So I shared mine with him. He didn't seem to mind the peach yogurt but refused to try any of the granola. My turkey on wheat with light mayo and lettuce was split in half, and both of us seemed to enjoy that most.

Now, we're outside. And let me just say the shift in temperature is more than I think any of us were prepared for. The cool spring air from yesterday turned abruptly to sweltering

heat that made breathing difficult even if you didn't have ail-
ments like asthma, which, coincidentally, Jill Cooper does.
Lucky for her—because of that, she was allowed to stay in the
building while we continue to hike through the thin patch of
trees down to the lake.

The purpose is to observe the wetland ecosystems by con-
ducting net and water sampling. We're supposed to test for
temperature, dissolved oxygen and pH. But really, we're just
walking. Mr. Emory's in the front of the group, talking about
something. I can hear his voice, but I'm not really paying attention. I'm in the back, supposedly making sure we don't have
any stragglers. But since I'm so hot and so uncomfortable, I
feel like straggling behind myself.

It's nearing two o'clock, which is good because we have to
be back at the Nature Center to board the bus at two-thirty.
The trees break, and we're in the clearing, just a few feet away
from where the lake ripples and flows out into the Atlantic
Ocean. The water's dark and murky-looking, and for a minute
I think I can see bubbles, like it's boiling.

But that's just silly.

Our group of twenty students and one teacher spread out
along the bank, gathering in small groups of like three or
four.

"We'd better at least act like we're working," Jake comes
up beside me and says.

"Yeah, I guess so," I agree, reaching into my pocket to pull
out the plastic gloves Mr. Emory gave us all at the start of the
trip.

Krystal has her gloves on and already has tweezers as she
moves about looking on the ground.

"We should get closer to the water," Antoine says.

"Why?" I ask.

"If you want to get good samples for the pH, they're going to be closer to the water."

For a minute I almost ask how he knows. Antoine isn't in any of the gifted and talented classes. Actually, his classes are for below grade level students. Usually the ones where they just push kids through high school to get rid of them. But as I listen to him, I have to admit he sounds like he knows what he's talking about. Maybe everything I thought was true about Antoine really isn't.

"Okay, let's go."

Me and Antoine move closer to the water, and the bubbling I thought I saw before is now full-fledged splashing. I instantly look out towards where I hear the sounds. "Do you hear that?"

"Hear what?" Antoine asks from beside me.

"That. The splashing, like something's out there."

I don't hear his response, but I assume he's shaking his head negatively. I'm hearing and seeing things again. I've got to remember that Antoine isn't one of us. He doesn't have any supernatural powers and no radar for the freaky unnatural stuff that's happening in this town.

But then Krystal's right beside me. "Something's out there," she says.

"No way," Franklin chimes in. "I mean, unless you mean some old bass and maybe some bottom-feeders. That's all that's in this old lake."

I sense something else. I keep staring, and just when I think to turn away, the something I've sensed shoots up from the water, sprinkling all of us as it does.

Krystal and I jump back, the guys mumble a few curses, then we all stand speechless, watching as it floats toward us.

* * *

As dead bodies go, I think this is the most disgusting thing I've ever seen. It looks deformed, all fat in places and sopping wet in others. The skin on the face is purple and looks like the bottom of an old tennis shoe. And if that isn't enough, the eyes, or should I say the sockets, are empty. And by empty I mean, where the eyes should have been, there are dug-out holes. Something crawls out of the left one, and I turn, ready to puke up my lunch.

Antoine is right there, his hands on my shoulders as I lean forward and turn. "Don't look anymore." I can hear him talking, but I'm studiously obeying his words and not looking. At anything.

After we saw the body floating, me and Krystal's combined screams alerted the rest of the group. Mr. Emory ushered us all back a few feet while using his cell phone to call the police. The police arrived complete with news crews and the county coroner's black van.

My eyes are closed while I try getting the picture of dead-no-eye-guy out of my mind. But that's all everyone is talking about. Including Alyssa, who I've been trying to avoid on this trip.

"Really, Sasha. It's not that bad," she says in an exasperated voice.

I don't even have the energy to rebut. It is that bad, but Alyssa wouldn't know that. She wouldn't know because I'm a hundred percent positive she didn't see the dark shadow floating just above the water where the body emerged.

It was there as I looked at them removing the body. A long dark arm reaching out toward me, as if beckoning me to come closer. I didn't, of course, but I need to find out if the other Mystyx saw it, if the dark shadow is calling all of us. Or if, for some insane reason, I've been singled out.

Antoine is still right on my heels when I start walking toward the spot beneath the trees where Jake stands, hands stuck in his pockets, eyes glued to the water. Lindsey isn't there. This wasn't her field trip, I remember while I'm moving toward Krystal, who's looking around frantically.

"Have you seen Franklin?" is what she says the moment I walk up to her.

"No," I answer immediately because it's true. Ever since the first scream I think everybody's attention became riveted on the water. "I thought he was with you."

Krystal's ponytail is swishing back and forth as she shakes her head. "He was. Then we heard the scream, he turned and I turned. And then he was gone."

I lean a little closer to Krystal and lower my voice so Antoine can't hear me over all the other noise around us. Most of the kids are on cell phones, probably telling their parents that instead of collecting foliage samples, we found a dead body.

"Did you see the shadow?"

At first she looks at me weirdly, then her eyes kind of dart around to make sure we won't be heard. I don't know why because she doesn't speak her answer, just nods her head.

Whew. I feel better knowing I'm not alone in this. "Did Jake see it, too?"

"Think so," Krystal says quickly. "I wonder where Franklin could have gone."

She returns to her search for Franklin, which kind of rubs me the wrong way. I mean, really, where could he have gone? We have a serious problem making itself known. I think she needs to focus more on that. But then Jake startles us both with his next comment.

"Let him go. You can do better than him anyway."

Both me and Krystal look at him strangely. Then I almost

strain my neck, turning to look at Antoine, who follows up Jake's remark with, "I know that's right."

"What? Well, that's just great. Thanks for your opinion," Krystal says to Jake, then looks over my shoulder to Antoine. "And yours, too."

She stalks off, and I give Jake a "what are you doing?" look, but he just shrugs. I don't give Antoine any kind of look. I just go after Krystal.

"Hey, don't take what they say seriously. They're just guys."

"Yeah, whatever," she says, but she's looking out at the water.

So I look out there, too.

"What are you thinking?" I ask when the silence between us is becoming just as nerve-wracking as the siren on the police car and all the other chatter going on around that dead body.

"I'm thinking something's not right."

"With the dead body?"

"The body. The shadow." She grows quiet again, and I look at her. She looks like she sees something.

Krystal can see, hear and talk to ghosts. So it isn't unusual for her to stare off like something's there that nobody else sees. Only she hasn't done that in a couple weeks, not that I know of.

"He was dragged here," she starts saying, but she's whispering.

I move a little closer to her, still trying to act like we're doing nothing more but looking out to the water. "Who was?"

"The boy. His name's David Sutherby. He was on that bus with the other kids, the ones that went on the retreat."

"So somebody dragged him here and drowned him?"

Krystal shakes her head negatively. "*Something* dragged him here, gouged out his eyes, then tossed him in the river."

The minute her last word is out, there's a huge gust of air. I mean so huge that it knocks both of us flat on our butts. Antoine and Jake both come running.

"What are you doing down here?" Jake's asking, grabbing Krystal under her arms and pulling her up.

Antoine comes up beside me doing the same. "Did you fall over each other?"

"No. It was the wind," Krystal started saying, but from the look on Jake and Antoine's faces, they hadn't felt that little breeze.

So that means it's supernatural. Which also means I have to get rid of Antoine or risk him asking way too many questions, or worse, finally realizing our differences go way beyond the black and white.

"Um, I think we saw something down here. Something the cops should see. Could you go and get them?" I ask, turning in his arms to face him.

He looks a little reluctant but then shrugs and says, "Sure."

As soon as he's out of earshot, I turn back to Jake and Krystal. "What the hell was that?"

"A warning, I think," Krystal says, brushing off her clothes.

Jake's still standing close to her, even though he's no longer touching her. Krystal looks more than a little angry with Jake, but again, now is not the time to be going over trivial stuff such as Jake liking Krystal but being too afraid to tell her and Krystal being too wrapped up in Franklin to see it.

"What are you talking about? The dead body?"

"The dead body came from that busload of kids that went

missing. Something dragged him here, took his eyes and killed him." I give Jake a quick version.

To his credit, he doesn't look like he doubts my words. "How do we know for sure?"

Or maybe not.

"A spirit came to me," Krystal says. "She's really worried about things she's seen happen along the waterfront lately."

"Did she tell you who did this to him?"

Krystal shakes her head. "It wasn't a 'who.' She said some 'thing.'"

"You think it's the Darkness?" I ask.

"I think it's connected," Krystal says.

Jake nods. "Definitely connected."

He's looking around now like he expects another body to pop up out of the water.

And that's exactly what happens.

Only this body is alive, kicking and flailing like a drowning victim.

"Help!"

The word is quickly swallowed up by water as the person goes under again.

Krystal and I immediately run to the water's edge, but Jake pushes us both aside. Before the cops or any of the other students or anyone from the news crew that have just arrived could come to our aid, Jake is wading through the shallow end of the water until he has no choice but to swim out.

Antoine, who I thought was still over there with the cops, surprises me by going in, too. He and Jake swim side by side until they reach the person who had popped back up through the surface like a wayward buoy.

It's when they get him to the shore that Krystal gasps. "Franklin."

Instantly falling to her knees, she looks down at Franklin's soaked clothes and color-drained face. "Ohmygod, what happened? How'd you get in the water?"

She's talking to him, but Franklin is too busy spitting up the icky green-tinted water that filled his lungs.

"Just hold on, man," Antoine says, looking around. "The medics are coming over this way."

And he's right. A few seconds later, medics swarm us, pushing all of us out of the way so they can work on Franklin.

Krystal stares down at the spot where he was, even though she can't see him through the circle of people working on him. She looks worried and scared, so I put an arm around her.

"He's going to be fine. He's puking up everything he swallowed so he'll be able to breathe just fine in a few minutes."

"How did he get in there?" she asks quietly.

"I don't know," I answer, but then I hear this deep laughter. It echoes around me, starting slow, then building as if someone's watching a scene from a movie that is just too hilarious to do anything else but laugh.

I'm instantly freaked because I know nobody but me hears this. I keep my eyes rooted to the ground just like Krystal because I know that if I look up, if I search for it, I'll find it.

I'll find what's haunting us.

# twelve

"We should do something, Marvin. Why weren't they chaperoned? Why wasn't somebody else there to find that body?"

My mother is hysterical. If it weren't for the fact that I'd never seen her look this on edge, her dark brown eyes wide with shock and repulsion, I could probably feel sorry for her. As it stands, I'm just tired of her dramatic performance. I've been home for a little over an hour, and already police officers have been here to inform my parents of what happened at the lake. Even though there was no need—I would have eventually gotten around to telling them. Maybe sometime next year.

This is exactly the scene I didn't want to have to sit through. But here I am in the den, my back cushioned by the many decorative pillows on the Australian couch. My feet were propped on the corner of the cherrywood table until my mother had given me a stern glance—right between her tirade about the safety of her child and the inconsideration of the authorities to allow dead bodies to float around in public areas. Yep, she said *they*—the authorities—were inconsiderate. Could she be more shallow? Or more dense? I can't figure out which one I'd rather blame it on.

"Calm down, Lidia. The police arrived as soon as they were dispatched. And I've already spoken to Chief Daniels.

He's going to make sure we have extra patrolmen around Sea Point for the next week or so. We're perfectly safe here."

"I don't know," she says, wringing her hands and pacing like an addict who needs a fix.

"Can I go now?" I say because this is just too much for even me to take. It's like some form of punishment for something I didn't even do.

I mean, really, I didn't kill that boy. I didn't gouge his eyes out and toss him in the lake. I was just there when they pulled him out. When the Darkness decided to show him to us.

And then there was Franklin. How had he gotten into the water? And why did he look like someone or something had scared ten years off his young life when the paramedics finished pumping the water out of his lungs?

Too many questions. Not enough answers.

I sigh and stand. "I have homework."

My father's rubbing his smooth chin, looking at me as if he just met me ten minutes ago. "It's Friday night," he says like he thinks I don't already know that.

I guess it is weird that a teenager would actually want to do homework on a Friday night. But when the homework actually consists of researching astral planes and wicked dark beings, that changes things significantly.

"Killer test on Monday," I say, shrugging and heading toward the door.

My mother makes this panicked-like sound and slumps into the wingback chair that just happens to be right behind her. She's fanning her own face, and it takes everything in me not to sigh and say, "give it up already." Instead I just shake my head and keep walking.

"Sasha."

I have no choice but to stop at the sound of my father's authoritative voice.

When I turn back to face him, I can see he's waiting expectantly. I swear, sometimes it's like living with an alien family around here. "Yes, sir?" I answer in a tone that's low and borderline exasperated.

"I have something for you to do tonight. You can do homework tomorrow."

Oh no, this is not going to be good. How can I tell? Maybe it's the bottom that feels like it's just dropped out of my stomach. Or how about the way my mother sits up in the chair—fanning her face has ceased, and her eyes look a little brighter. Miraculous recovery or something up the parental sleeves? I'll bet my trust fund on the latter.

"Stephen Whitman the Fourth owns several oil rigs and a huge company in Texas. For health reasons, he and his family had to relocate here to Lincoln about a year or so ago."

Yes, I know Stephen Whitman IV. His parents ship him off to some private school in upstate New York all year long. I think there's an older sister too, in college maybe. But what this has to do with me remains to be seen. So I keep quiet and wait. Not an easy task for me, so I'm shuffling from one foot to the other, anxious to have this over with so I can be gone.

"The young Stephen Whitman is home for spring break. I told his parents you would love to go out with him tonight, show him around town a bit."

"You what?" The words just roll out. I don't know who is more shocked, me or my mother. Certainly my father, by the rise of his eyebrows, was taken aback. "I mean, what does that mean?" I have a sinking feeling what it meant.

"I've made reservations at Solange for the two of you. Mr. Lycanian will drive you."

My parents always call Mouse, "Mr. Lycanian." But from

the first day I met him, he'd instructed me to call him Mouse. So that's what I did.

"I don't want to go to dinner with Stephen Whitman the Fourth," I say in protest, knowing already that it's pointless.

"Life is not about what we want, Sasha. It's about what's best for us, for our family, our legacy. Want rarely comes into play."

What he really means is that want rarely comes into play where I'm concerned. My parents seem to have everything their chilly little hearts desire. Me, on the other hand, well, let's just say I'm not like my parents. Some days I wake up and even consider requesting a DNA test.

My mother's still jabbering. "He's a handsome boy, Sasha. I think you two will really hit it off."

"His father's thinking of investing considerably in the new club," my father adds, as if that should be enough to send me on my way.

"Then you go out with him!" I say again on impulse. It must be the adrenaline still rushing through my system. I mean, it's not every day a girl watches a body being dragged from the lake. I had to have some excuse for mouthing off to my parents. Especially to my father.

Well clearly, Marvin Carrington is having none of that, regardless of my reasoning.

"You will do as I tell you, young lady. You're a part of this family and will act accordingly." His normally cool green eyes grow just a tad darker as his voice rises.

I feel like I've been slapped, even though neither one of them have ever put their hands on me. Not even for a hug that I can remember. Then I bristle at his words. *Now* I'm a part of this family. What happened to consoling their teenage daughter who had just been through a horrific time? What happened to wanting to keep her safe? Clearly there's a killer on the loose.

While I'm standing here thinking all this and literally biting my tongue to keep from mouthing off some more, my mother stands and walks over to me. "You don't go out with enough guys, dear. This will be fun."

Was she kidding? What mother tells her fifteen-year-old daughter, "you don't go out with enough guys?" Normally, it's exactly the opposite. This place is like a freak show.

"I don't feel like having fun." And I really don't. Not with some strange guy anyway. This just cannot be happening.

"Now, just go on upstairs. Casietta already has something picked out for you to wear. Stephen will be here in an hour. Take a nice long bath and do your hair. Oh, you're going to have a fabulous time."

She's rubbing my back with one hand, the other is doing something weird to my hair, and her voice is like chalk scraping down a blackboard. I want to scream.

"And Sasha…"

I look over my shoulder to see my father not even looking up at me but shuffling some papers around in a folder he's been holding on his lap. "Be sure to talk up the club. How you and your friends will be spending a lot of time there and such."

Yeah, I think when I'm finally allowed to leave the room with the two psycho parents in it, I'll talk up the club that I never plan to set foot in. Stomping up the steps seems juvenile, but I do it anyway, releasing only minute waves of frustration as I go.

I'm not their daughter. I'm a pawn in this game of their lives. They don't care what I do or how I feel as long as everything works out for them.

I shouldn't care about what they want or how they'll feel if I do something they don't like. I shouldn't.

But I do.

It's pathetic, but I do care. I do want their approval. So I take the shower and I get dressed and I wait for the date I don't want to go on in the hopes that one day things between us will be different.

His pants are too high.

That's the first thing I notice about Stephen Whitman IV. And that's probably because I can see his argyle socks as he walks toward me. His khaki pants are hard creased and swing at his ankles like they're boot cut. His shoes are leather, Italian probably. I keep looking at them because, of course, I'm a shoe-aholic.

"Hi, Sasha," he says when he's closer, his hand already extended for me to shake like we're closing a business deal or something.

I sigh, then force a smile. My hand lifts and embraces his, but I swear it must be on autopilot because that's not what I was thinking of doing. I'm actually considering turning and running back up the stairs. This night isn't going to go off as planned. I can feel it deep down in my bones.

"Hi, Stephen."

"You look beautiful."

Do boys say *beautiful?* More importantly, do they really mean it when they say it? Probably not.

"Thanks," is my automatic response.

"Shall we go?"

My parents already had the opportunity to talk to him, filling his mind with a bunch of crap about their precious club, I presume. But I'd stayed upstairs a little longer than necessary, especially since I'd seen when the Rolls Royce pulled around to the front of the house and watched as the suited driver stepped out and opened the back door for Stephen.

I'd known he was here and still hid upstairs like a Chicken Little. But hey, I'm not even afraid to admit that. I don't want to go on this date. And for some reason, the not wanting is a little more adamant than just not liking Stephen. I really feel like this is going to end badly.

Well, too late now.

My arm is already threaded through Stephen's, and we're stepping out the door into the cool night air. And I do mean cool, like it's dropped about ten degrees since earlier this afternoon at the lake. But that's the way the weather is here in Lincoln—strange.

Solange is located on the first floor of the Nokland Hotel. It's a pretty jazzed-up place complete with huge chandeliers with dripping tiers of crystal lights, linen tablecloths and soft, high-backed chairs. Walking across the dark maroon carpeted floor, my feet slide a bit because these shoes are new. I bought them out of a catalog which I don't do often, but I needed a new pair of patent leather shoes with the kitten heel, and these have a cute white bow on the side toe end. The skirt Casietta picked out for me is pleated black with a white cami and midriff sweater to match. I feel like I should be going to church instead of on a date. I know I wouldn't have to dress like this to go out with Antoine.

"So how's school?" Stephen asks after we're seated.

For the first time since he picked me up I really look at his face. He's not half bad looking, if you like the straitlaced, pretty-boy type. I mean, his hair is cut low, he has like a semi-tan. He probably goes to the beach over the long weekends. Either that or a tanning salon, but I don't really see one of the Whitmans visiting Teri's Tanning Tub every week. His eyes are blue and his hair is blond—clichéd, but true. There are some highlights to his hair at the top that make it look a little darker than it is on the sides, might be from the sun. Still, his clothes are perfectly starched. His Rolex watch shines at his wrist, and what I think is a gold school ring twinkles on his left ring finger. He's sitting with his back bone-straight in the chair and at this very moment unfolding his napkin and placing it, sort of daintily, in his lap.

Like I said, fine if you like the straitlaced, pretty-boy type.

I definitely do not.

"School is school," I reply rather blandly. I never really know how to answer this question. Plus I think it's one of the stupidest questions to ask a teenager. What's really the expected response—"School is great!" or "School sucks!"? Some days I can say either one, but I kind of like the answer I just gave.

"You're in the tenth grade, right?"

"Yes."

He nods his head, then picks up the menu. "I remember those days."

"What grade are you in?"

"Eleventh."

Yeah, so he remembers the tenth-grade days like they were five or so years ago. Please, somebody, save me from this brutally boring evening!

And just like that my phone chimes in my purse. I'm receiving a text.

# thirteen

Who's the geek?

It's Antoine. I try to hide my smile.

"Important?" Stephen asks, looking at me around the wide menu.

I almost forget he's there. So I look up at him, give him a fraction of the attention I probably should, considering he's my date. "Ah, yeah. My friend Krystal. She's still freaking about this afternoon. Just gonna try and calm her down," I say, then start texting Antoine back.

where r u?

Because he has to be close. He knows I'm with somebody, a geek he said. Smile can't be held back this time.

close. answer my ?
a friend
a close friend?

Aww, he sounds jealous. Or the message has a jealous tone I guess. My heart skips a little beat at that. Fingers are already flying over the keypad.

just met him 2day
I would have bought u dinner
not hungry. bored.
☺

Except for the smiley, there's no other response. I stare at the phone for a few more minutes but no reply.

Stephen finally clears his throat. "Ah, is she okay now? Do you want to order?"

"Oh," I say and reluctantly stuff my phone back into my purse. "Yeah. Sure." Picking up the menu, I scan both sides. I haven't been here in a while. Family dinners out aren't really a part of my parents' daily plans. But it's not too hard to find something I like.

"I'll have the charbroiled beef with cheddar cheese, lettuce, tomato and mayonnaise and a baked potato." That's the closest this fancy-smancy restaurant is going to get to a cheeseburger and fries.

The waiter appears, and Stephen repeats my order, then follows with his own. "I'll have the seared sea bass, steamed asparagus and rice pilaf."

I feel like I'm having dinner with a grown-up. I mean, come on, it's Friday night, we're on a date, alone, and he orders fish and veggies. I wonder how many other strikes in the "abso-freakin-lutely not" column he's going to rack up.

"So you saw a dead body." He starts another conversation after the waiter leaves. "That must have been upsetting."

"That's an understatement," I respond even though lately, I've seen worse.

"Do you know who it was?"

"Rumor has it one of the kids from that missing bus." Well, at least the rumor would have it. I mean, I know from another source. But Tessa Jermain's dad is the chief of police, so I know she'll be blabbing every detail she can overhear the minute she overhears them.

"Hmm. You think the other kids are dead, too?"

I shrug, hoping that's not the case.

"A killer in Lincoln, that seems so odd."

"Why? A killer was arrested just a few weeks ago," I say, thinking about Mr. Lyle.

"Yeah, odd. Lincoln isn't known for its violence, yet suddenly there are vicious murders taking place. Probably a result of more lower-class people migrating here from the city. They think life will be easier here, cheaper. But we're the ones who have to suffer for it. They're invading our neighborhoods and hampering our lifestyles. That's why this club of your father's is such a good idea. A place where we can all band together, a place where they aren't welcome."

My whole body is vibrating with rage that heightens with each word he speaks. I want to close my eyes and disappear. Just leave his prejudiced boring ass at this table talking to himself. Instead I pick up the glass of water, concentrate on the coolness in my hand and not the emerging idea of throwing the water in his face. After taking a slow sip, I speak with as much calm as I can muster.

"It's a free country. Anybody can live wherever they want. And rich people kill, too. What about those boys that killed that girl on her spring break in Aruba?"

Stephen's already shaking his head in disagreement. "Totally different circumstances. These killings seem random."

"There was nothing random about killing the girls who threatened to tell Mr. Lyle was a pervert. Or killing the boy who was either going to the police with the evidence or going to kick his butt. Mr. Lyle deserved to get caught. And whoever did this to that boy in the water will be caught too because they deserve to be in jail. Regardless of how much money they have."

He doesn't move, just sits with his napkin in his lap staring at me. "You have a lot to learn, but the club will help you with that."

What's that supposed to mean?

"The club is not going to be a school," I say and roll my eyes at him.

"No, but it'll be a place where we can bond, learn to stick together in this town. There're some unsavory elements moving in and it's up to us to get them out."

My mouth opens to say something else to him but then someone stops me.

"Good evening, Sasha."

Antoine steps up to the table, one hand in the front pocket of his crisp, baggy blue jeans. He wears a long-sleeved white button-down shirt that actually looks like he'd just purchased it tonight. His close-cut hair is brushed neatly, and his thick eyebrows arch just slightly as he turns to speak to Stephen.

"Antoine Watson," he says, extending his hand to Stephen for a shake.

Stephen, true to his stupid pretty-boy form, looks Antoine up and down, ignores his outstretched hand and says tightly, "Stephen Whitman the Fourth."

Antoine just nods his head like he really understands now and pulls his hand back. "Cool," he says, then looks back at me.

"Hungry?"

I smile, never being more happy to see someone in my life. "Starving."

"We've just ordered. Our food will be here in seconds. If you'll excuse us," Stephen says.

"Wrong," Antoine says and reaches a hand out to me. "*Your*

food will be here in a few seconds. Ours will come from someplace else. You can now excuse us."

My heart's beating at a rapid pace as I put my hand in Antoine's and stand. I'm leaving with him. Leaving stuck-up Stephen sitting there waiting for his asparagus spears.

"That's not possible," Stephen says, standing but being sure to grab the napkin from his lap and toss it on the table. "Sasha is my date for the evening."

I'm standing behind Antoine because, when he grabs my hand, he positions himself between me and Stephen in a protective kind of way. He shakes his head and gets close up on Stephen.

"But she's my girl all day, every day."

Stephen looks appalled. I want to dance around, sing a song, anything to show how happy I am at this moment. Instead, I simply shrug as I walk past Stephen's flabbergasted expression.

Antoine continues to walk out of the restaurant, not fast like he's trying to hurry up before Stephen decides to get up and make a scene. Probably because he knows Stephen has no backbone and would never do such a thing. But he takes his time, like if anybody wants to stop us they can certainly get up and try. I follow behind him dutifully, the smile on my face so wide, my cheeks might start to hurt soon.

Then we're outside, and Antoine hands the valet his little white ticket. I'm a little shocked, but then, you can't get into Solange without giving the valet your car to park. I guess I'm more shocked that they let Antoine in at all. Solange and the Nokland have a strict dress code—shirt, tie, slacks for men and skirts, dresses, etc. for women. Antoine is so out of line of the dress code with his boots, jeans and shirt. Still, he looks totally hot!

When his car arrives, he opens the door for me, and I slide

into the passenger seat. More shock registers as he actually leans in, reaches over me and buckles my seat belt.

"Better safe than sorry," he whispers, his face close to mine.

"Right," I murmur, but when he pulls back and closes the door, I curse my stupid tongue for making such an idiotic remark.

We drive in silence for about fifteen minutes. Me wondering if I should ask Antoine if he really meant what he said about me being his girl. Him, just driving, I guess. I can't tell if he's thinking something or not. But now I'm wondering where we're going, so I speak up.

"Where are you taking me?"

He doesn't look over at me, just makes the next left turn. "You said you were hungry," is his reply.

"Oh." I recognize the next street we turn down and figure out that we're heading to the mall.

Antoine turns into the garage and takes the keys out of the ignition. I unbuckle my seat belt and am reaching for the door handle to get out when he grabs my arm.

"If you're gonna be my girl, then dating other guys, especially geeks, has to stop."

His tone is serious, and I can see—even in the dark interior of the car—that his facial expression is, too.

"I didn't know I was your girl," I respond.

He exhales and lets his head fall back on the headrest. "Come on, Sasha. When are you going to stop acting like you don't know what's going on between us?"

"I don't know, Antoine. But since you seem to have all the answers, why don't you tell me?" I'm agitated now because I don't like that he's acting like he's tired of me playing with him. I guess he is. And maybe I am playing the dumb role because that keeps me from taking a stand either way.

"I want you to be my girl," he says then, and his voice is softer. He reaches out a hand and turns his head to stare at me. His fingers toy with the ends of my hair. "I like you and I want to be with you. I can't make it any simpler than that. So now it's on you. What do you want?"

Oh boy, it's on me all right. I feel like I'm in front of a room full of people, and I'm wearing only my panties and bra. It's just me and Antoine in this car, I keep telling myself. And I'm fully dressed. It's just that his question makes me seem naked, vulnerable, I mean. So I take a deep breath and release it slowly.

"I like you, Antoine."

"And?" he says expectantly.

I look right at him this time and know what I've been fighting these last few weeks is finished. I can't fight it anymore. He knows it, too.

"And I want to be with you."

His smile is slow but spreads wide, and my insides quiver. He leans over, and I know he's going to kiss me. I want this kiss so bad my lips part even before he's that close to me. The hand that was in my hair is now at the back of my neck, pulling me closer. I lean over the console, and then our faces are close enough. Our lips touch real soft once. And then again. And after that, the softness is mostly gone. This kiss is urgent like he's searching for something, or I am, one of us is.

I'm lost in the touch of his lips on mine, my mind is so wrapped around him that I forget we're in the car until he breaks the kiss. Both of us are breathing heavy when he rests his forehead against mine.

"Let's go and get you something to eat," he says.

I just nod my head, and before I can say anything, he's releasing me and getting out of the car.

I only have a few seconds before he's at my door opening

it for me, but in that time I take a few steadying breaths and figure I'm okay when I step out of the car and he takes my hand in his.

But we've only taken a couple steps, hand-in-hand, boy-friend and girlfriend, when I see it.

A dark form hovering around this man like a shadow. The man is walking fast to his car, bags in one hand, keys in the other. He's wearing dress shoes, and they click across the cement. The form follows him, attached to his every motion. I keep staring, even once the man is in his car and about to pull off. The form is gone with him, and I wonder if I imagined it. Then I hear the laughter—it's loud and echoes throughout the parking garage.

Antoine is still walking, his expression hasn't changed, and he hasn't said anything. He doesn't hear it. I know this. But I do.

I hear it, and I know what it is, what it wants.

And I'm afraid.

# fourteen

It's close to eight at night, and the mall is still crowded. They close at nine, but people are milling about like they have hours and hours more to shop.

We head straight to the escalators, avoiding all the stores on the lower level, and aim for the food court on level two. Antoine's still holding my hand, and I really like that. I guess we look like the other couples I'm seeing as we walk. Except some of them are really hugged up—I mean to the point that I'm ready to shout, "get a room!"

Still, I'm happy to be walking with my boyfriend. Happy that I now have a boyfriend. That makes me instantly think of Krystal and Franklin because now I can see that some of my irritation with them always being joined at the hip was because I didn't have anybody to join at the hip with. But now I do. I'm pleased.

Except my eyes are determined to play tricks on me. Right in front of the music store is a group of teenagers. The guys—three of them—all have on skinny jeans hanging off their butts to show their boxers. Don't ask me why this is a style. It's crazy to think that showing your underwear is cute.

There're two girls with them, both wearing leggings and short ruffled skirts. At first glance they look normal—whatever normal is for teenagers these days. The standard is always changing, it's a struggle to keep up. That's why sometimes I wish for the moment I can officially say I'm an adult and do my own thing.

Anyway, they look just like other groups of teens congregating, talking, not buying a thing, just hanging out. In which case I would have normally shrugged them off. Except this group did have one distinct difference—their faces aren't like normal teenagers.

The two girls have long, pale faces. Around their eyes are dark brown circles with lashes that don't look like they are using the store-bought mascara. Both of them have golden eyes and black marks on their face in some weird pattern. But it's their hair that really startles me. Snakes, that's exactly what the long, moving strands resemble.

And the boys, their lower bodies remain the same, but again their faces are different. Caved in at the cheeks so that they look more skeletal than human, and their complexion a dusty gray, and yet it's their eyes that have my heart thumping wildly. Or their lack of eyes, I should say. The pits where pupils should be are empty, dug out.

Just like the boy at the lake.

"Sasha!"

My head shakes once, twice. Then I jump as if waking up from a bad dream. Antoine is standing in front of me, his hands on each of my shoulders, shaking me.

"You okay?" he's asking as I look over toward the group of strange teens, then back at him.

They're still there, and they still look weird. "Huh?" I finally manage to answer.

"Are you okay? You zoned out for a minute, staring over there like you know one of them. You want to go speak?"

His voice sounds a little irritated. I lick my lips nervously. "Ah, no. No. I don't know them."

"Then why are you staring at them like that?"

"I don't know," I answer quickly and purposely keep my
head still and my eyes trained on Antoine so I won't look
at them again. "I'm fine. Let's eat," I say, hurrying to move
toward the food court.

At the only burger stand in the entire mall, Antoine orders
me a cheeseburger, fries and a root beer. For himself he gets
a big beef hot dog with every condiment they have dropped
onto it. We sit at one of the tables close to the wall and, for
the most part, eat in silence.

Until a girl comes up to the table.

"Hey, Twan. Haven't seen you in a while," she says.

I finish chewing my French fry and look up at her. The
voice is definitely feminine and the body is definitely all girl.
She's wearing a leather push-up bra and a matching swatch of
material that just barely covers her other vital parts.

"Hi, LaToya," Antoine says in a less than enthusiastic
voice.

"Why haven't you called me?" she asks.

Now he's even more irritated. "Can't you see I've got
company?"

"Oh," LaToya says, then she looks my way.

I almost fall out of the chair.

She's beautiful. I mean, picture-perfect beauty. Flawless
golden skin, hazel eyes, thick arched brows, perfect pouty lips
painted with a light lip gloss. Her hair is long, an auburn color,
rolling down her back in heavy ringlets. But on each side at
the top of her head like antennaa are two small horns.

I'm losing my mind. I have to be. There's something in the
air, some airborne virus that's affecting my sight. Or maybe
it's in the food, the brown bag lunch that was packed by Mrs.
Cullinson, the crazy cafeteria lady, and handed out on the field
trip this afternoon. Maybe it's something from the lake, like

poison ivy, or some other bacteria coming from the polluted water.

Or maybe...

Something clicks into place in my mind. Maybe...it's from going to that other plane. The one I can get to because of my astral projection power.

But I'm certainly not there now because Antoine is here. He's sitting right across from me in this crowded mall with all these other normal-looking people. But as I look past LaToya, I see that some of the people are normal and others...well, let's just say they aren't the face of the American people.

"I gotta go," I say quickly and stand up.

"What? Sasha, wait. You haven't finished eating."

"Yeah, I know. I just gotta get out of here."

LaToya just smiles at me like she knows I know what she really is. I wonder what Antoine sees. Probably just a perfectly stacked teenage girl, trying to get with him.

"Stay away from him," I get up in her face and warn. Then on impulse I push her. Hard. She falls back against the table, then looks straight at me, or through me.

She throws her head back and laughs, like the wicked witch in the *The Wizard of Oz*. Old and sick and cacklelike.

I start walking, and Antoine's right behind me. "Hey, what's your problem?"

"What's your problem?" I say, whirling on him. I raise my voice, and a few people look at us wondering what's going on.

Antoine takes a step back, lifting both his hands in the air like I told him he's under arrest or something. I turn and keep walking fast until I find the escalator and head down. I try not to look at anyone else because I don't want to see. Or I do want to see—if they're normal. But those other things I can do without.

I race ahead.

"I'll take you home," Antoine says from behind me when we get to the parking lot.

I expected him to be gone but hadn't turned around to confirm. I'm too afraid of seeing someone or some*thing* else. Now I feel like a colossal idiot. He's moving around to unlock the car door, not saying anything, and I'm standing here looking like a fool.

I can't believe I just freaked out like that. He probably thinks I'm a total geek. What can I say? How can I fix this?

"Well, are you going to get in?"

His words snap me out of my moments of self-pity. "Ah, yeah. Listen, I'm sorry about what happened back there. It's just that girl, she, um, she acted like you two knew each other."

He leans back against the car, just staring at me.

I know I need to keep going, I'm not really getting through to him. "I mean, like you two really *knew* each other. I felt like I was intruding." Which isn't exactly a lie. LaToya had totally ignored me until I all but jumped out of the chair at her.

"So you were jealous? Is that why you took off like that?"

He doesn't believe me. That's just great! Can this night be any more messed up? No, let me not even ask that question.

"I didn't know what else to do."

"Sitting there and continuing to eat would have been a good start." He sighs. "Look, I know Toya, and yeah, we used to kick it a while back. But not now. Not since I met you."

"Oh." Is all I can manage. "I'm sorry."

The corner of his mouth turns up in a smile. "It's cool. I don't think Toya's ever had anybody push her down the way you did. If she was trying to get at me, I think she got the message that I'm taken."

He sounds way too cocky, and I want to correct him, but I don't. Just letting the whole scene rest is the best option, I think.

"Whatever," I say, climbing into the front seat of his car once more.

"Like I said, it's cool," he says as he's leaning over me doing the seat belt thing again. "I like a girl who fights for what she wants. I think it's sexy," he says with a smile, then plants a quick kiss on my lips.

I'm too worked up from the scene and from the butterflies dancing around in my stomach at his touch to say anything else.

But on the ride home I think about all that's happened today and all that's to come. I don't like any of it.

The thing about going to Settleman's High is that it's the only high school in Lincoln. That means every teenager in town goes here. So just about everybody knows each other and in turn knows each other's business.

It's real irritating sometimes.

Like today.

"Heard you ditched Stephen Whitman the Fourth Friday night. Big mistake. I mean, major, major error in the dating arena."

Of course this is Alyssa who, ever since the dinner party at my house, has started hanging out at my locker in the mornings. Her quest for a new BFF is apparent. However, I'm almost positive I don't want it to be me.

"Stephen's an ass," I say, slamming my locker, maneuvering my books in one arm and balancing my new kaleidoscope Coach pouch on the other shoulder. The turquoise, green and white colors in my purse match perfectly with my white capris, turquoise tank and white flats with turquoise paisley design.

But if I thought I was casually, if moderately expensively, coordinated on this Monday morning, Alyssa certainly has me outdone. The short denim dress she's wearing is Dolce & Gabbana, and it's not actually denim, it's sort of a silky material, but has that stone-washed look. Her cocoa brown legs are bare to the intricately stitched cowboy boots on her feet. The boots match her bag, and her gold hoop earrings match the Chanel bracelet on her arm. Talk about flaunting your wealth.

The majority of the students at Settleman's are what I guess people would call middle class. They aren't shuffling for public funds to pay their bills, but work every day to support themselves and their families. A small percentage are a little better off, and even a smaller percentage of them like to show off. Alyssa included.

"Yeah, but he's a rich, well-connected ass. You know he's already been accepted into Duke and Harvard. His father owns Whitman Communications, one of, if not the largest wireless communication companies in the world. You know he's going to be set when he graduates."

"Set to lead a boring, mapped-out-for-him life. No thanks, I'd rather fly solo." I've already started walking down the hall, weaving my way through kids trying to get to class, or kids thinking about ditching class. Alyssa is still beside me chattering away, to my dismay.

Why did Camy have to bail? I mean, hey, I know she was mega embarrassed that she'd been letting Pervert Lyle take pictures of her nude and all, but couldn't she have stayed in town just to keep Alyssa company? That would have saved me a dozen or so headaches.

"Oh, okay, so riding off into the sunset with that poor, scruffy hoodlum Antoine is the better option."

Alyssa knows too much. She runs her mouth too much, and her basic existence is riding right along the lines of *too much!*

I stop, turn and glare at her. "Stay out of my personal business, Alyssa."

"Oooooh." She fakes being scared, tossing her rail thin arms up in the air and widening her already big brown eyes. "Is that a threat? What are you going to do if I don't stay out of your business, Sasha? Who are you going to tell? Your mom? Your dad? Oh, I forgot, they don't want you with that cretin any more than I do."

My fingers are clinching my books. "What? How do you know what my parents feel about Antoine?"

Alyssa moves her head so that her long braids fall gloriously over her right shoulder. Her smile turns syrupy sweet, and her voice lowers so that only I can hear her over the chattering kids in the hallway.

"Who do you think told them that Antoine whisked you away from a four-star restaurant to a lovely grease-filled burger joint at the mall?"

At that moment I'm itching to slap her, but the bell rings. So instead I just roll my eyes and stomp down the hall toward my Honors Literature class. Once I make it to the room, I take my seat near the window, dropping my books and my purse down on the desk, then plopping into the chair. I'm not in the mood for Mrs. Powell's lesson, no matter how much I usually enjoy this class. I want to go home. No, I don't because I remember the huge fight me and my parents had when I got home Friday night and now I know the reason for it.

Alyssa.

"Oh thank God, we were about to call the police," my mother had said the moment I closed the front door behind me.

My father was right on her heels, his stern look beating down on me with the intensity of a long leather belt.

"You want to explain to me how you managed to leave this house with Stephen Whitman the Fourth and returned with…" He hesitated and took a deep breath—at which time the tips of his ears and his cheeks turned a flaming red color. "Returned with that person," he said very tightly, like the words had to be forced out of his mouth.

I was caught. I knew it, but after all that I'd seen today, I didn't really care. "Stephen was being a jerk, so a friend of mine brought me home instead."

"That's not the way Stephen tells it," my mother interrupted. "Poor Stephanie was so upset when she called." Stephanie was Stephen's mother. I know, it's sickening, right? All their names beginning with *S*. A bigger group of pompous airheads I'd never met before.

"She said Stephen was beside himself when he arrived home. He was actually afraid for your life. Said this thug came and took you away."

My mother had said *thug* like it was the mother of all curse words. She'd actually frowned her perfect-no-wrinkle face and twisted her lips when she'd spoken.

"Who was he?" my father demanded to know.

I could have lied, but figured since they obviously already knew so much, why bother. "His name's Antoine Watson."

"Where does he live?"

I shifted from one foot to the other, not really wanting to say, but knowing I'd have to. "Bolten Street, I think," I said softly.

My mother instantly clutched her heart and stumbled back. It's almost funny that nobody moved to catch or assist her. My father actually cut her a weary look. I just stood, still praying this interrogation would hurry up so I could go to bed.

"That is not acceptable, Sasha. We are the Carringtons. We have an image to uphold. What would my backers in the club think if they knew you were running around with such, such…"

"Such what?" I prompted because I wanted to hear my father say it. I wanted to hear his prejudiced lips spit out some ridiculous typecast word that he believed described a boy he'd never met.

His lips closed tightly, and he took a step towards me. It took all the anger I was feeling at that moment to hold myself still. Because actually, on any other day, at any other time, the deadly look in my father's eyes would have had me running up the steps or out of the house, whichever would have kept me out of his reach.

"You. Will. Not. Be. Seen. With. Him. Again."

Each word was spoken like its own newspaper headline. Either he thought I was too stupid to comprehend regular speech, or he was trying to make a point.

My mother was wringing her hands and babbling something in Spanish. I didn't even try to translate because I just didn't care that much.

Just like they obviously didn't care about me.

"Whatever," I said and moved quickly past both of them.

"And you're grounded," my father shouted as I took the first couple of stairs.

Grounded? After what I'd seen today, that's the least of my worries.

# fifteen

"The first written literary work of ancient Greece is the *Iliad*. It was written by Homer around a thousand years before Christ."

"So this Homer's like really old, huh?"

My thoughts shift back from my crappy weekend to the topic Mrs. Powell just introduced and Jaeden March's smart-ass remark. Jaeden is super smart, so much so that he really doesn't need to sit in these classes to pass. He just, like, knows everything. That means he's bored most of the time and figures we all need his comic relief to get us through.

This time, even though some of the other kids in the class chuckle, I'm actually interested in what Mrs. Powell has to say.

"Yes, he would be by today's count," Mrs. Powell concedes. She's a tall woman, with a butter yellow complexion. Her hair is like this funny red color, and she always wears it in one thick braid down her back. "But more importantly, what I want us to look at in this study of Homer's work is how old the earth is, how long mankind has been around and some of the issues they faced back then that we're still facing today."

"We don't have to walk around being afraid of pissing Zeus off and him shoving a lightning bolt up our—"

Mrs. Powell holds up a hand at the precise moment Jaeden

is about to take his joking to another level entirely. The class giggles. I just shake my head.

"As usual, you're jumping ahead of me, Jaeden. Let's start at the beginning," Mrs. Powell says and passes out a packet of stapled papers. The title is "*The Iliad* of Homer."

It's not too thick, maybe about thirty pages. Surely this isn't the whole book. We've never read anything this small in this class.

"Now, before we start reading, I want to give you a little background." She moves to her podium and flips a few pages, slipping on stylish gold wire frames and looking down for a minute. Then she peers up over the rim of her glasses. "I know I don't have to tell you to take notes."

But yeah, she had to, because right after she says that, I flip open my notebook to a clean sheet of paper and grab a pen from my purse. The shuffling of papers behind me says that the other kids are taking her hint as well.

"Now, has anyone ever heard of the 'Greek miracle'?"

The question goes unanswered.

Mrs. Powell just keeps right on talking. "This phrase can be translated to 'Old things are passed away; behold, all things are become new.'"

"Not very good English, Mrs. Powell." Again with Jaeden's remarks.

"Not a very good idea for you to continue interrupting me, Mr. March."

At that I do laugh.

"As I said, the plan for this assignment is to make comparisons of how the 'old things passed away,' namely the timeless tales of gods and heroes, manifested into the 'all things become new.' To do that we're going to read Homer's *Iliad* and learn all about the ancient Greeks' ideas about the battle between good and evil, light and dark."

My fingers still at her last words, my pen suspended just over the paper. I can't write because what she's just said strikes something in me. I hurry up and flip to the first page of my packet and start reading, not really knowing what I'm searching for but believing instinctively that some of the answers I've been searching for might be in Homer's words.

"I had a vision last night," Krystal says when we all meet up in the hallway after school. I didn't go to lunch today so I hadn't sat with them, nor had I had the opportunity to tell them about what I saw Friday night at the mall.

"Really? What was it like?" This was Lindsey who wore leggings and a long rainbow tie-dyed shirt with a huge peace sign on its back.

Lindsey is still trying to learn as much about our powers as she can. She's like a really inquisitive three-year-old asking question after question. But it's cool. I so understand the need for answers.

Krystal shifts her books from one arm to the other and is reaching into her purse as she answers, "Like a dream but I'm completely awake. Sometimes it takes my breath away, depending what I see. This time, though, I was stunned for a couple seconds."

Krystal answers her cell phone, but there doesn't seem to be anybody on the line.

Lindsey nods, adding what Krystal said to her mental database. Jake walks a couple steps behind us. I hear him sigh. He really doesn't have any patience these days. I hope that doesn't trigger his powers to go all funky again. The last time he was feeling edgy and the opportunity presented itself, he busted Mateo Hunter and Pace Livingston's kneecaps with a two-by-four piece of wood, then psyched both the jocks out by playing with the locks on their doors. We don't want everyone to know about our powers, so keeping Jake's emotions—and therefore his powers—in check is a high priority.

"So what did you see?" he asks.

"It was weird. I mean they were weird. All these creatures walking around as if they belonged here, on earth."

I stop walking. "Creatures?"

They all stop. "Yeah," Krystal answers.

"Like girls with horns in their heads or snakes for hair? Boys with grotesque faces?"

Krystal nods. "You saw them, too?"

I nod.

"Where?" Jake inquires.

"How?" Lindsey chimes in.

"I don't know how. But I was at the mall and everywhere I turned they were there. These creatures."

Jake frowns. "Did anybody else see them?"

I shake my head. "No. I'm pretty sure I was the only one who could see their differences. One girl came right up to the table to talk to Antoine and he talked back to her as if she looked regular. But when I looked at her, I could see the differences."

"Wow," Lindsey sighs. "I wonder why you can see them and nobody else can."

"I think it has something to do with my astral projection. I mean with the other plane I can go to."

"You're saying there's another plane besides earth?" Jake asks.

"I think so."

"A plane where creatures exist," Krystal says slowly.

"Maybe a plane where the Darkness originated."

Jake is shaking his head. "Doesn't explain how or why we got our powers."

"No," I interject. "But it does get us one step closer. Plus, we all know that the Darkness is trying to tell us something. And that witch, Fatima, is trying to warn us about something. I think it's time we found out what."

"I agree, but I've got to go straight home today. My dad wants to talk to me about something. Says it's important." Jake hunches his shoulders like he doesn't care either way what his father has to say. Jake and his dad aren't close. Then again, what teenager is close to their parents? I know I'm certainly not. Krystal might be with her mom, but I know for a fact she still keeps her stepfather at arm's length. And Lindsey, well, we haven't found out that much about her yet.

"Okay, then just the ladies will work on it today," I say as we come to the break in the front hallway of the school where either you're going out the front doors to where the buses are or the side door to the parking lot.

"Actually," Lindsey says, looking at Jake then back at us. "I have to go right home, too. I'll take the bus with Jake."

To my surprise, Jake doesn't say anything against her suggestion. Maybe he's getting used to Lindsey, finally. Krystal's cell phone rings again.

"So are you cool to do some investigating this afternoon?" I ask her as she's staring at the screen on her phone with a confused look on her face.

She's nodding her head positively even as she puts the phone to her ear.

"God, doesn't he have anything better to do than keep calling her?" Jake says and stalks off towards the front doors.

Lindsey shrugs. "I'll try to talk to him," she says and I nod my head in agreement.

Both Jake and Lindsey are gone and it's just me and Krystal

standing in the hall. Krystal's yelling, "Hello? Hello?" into her phone again. I remember the strange calls she was getting a few weeks ago from Pervert Lyle and get concerned.

"Who was it?" I say when she clicks off and starts heading for the side door with me.

"Weird," she says. "It was definitely Franklin's number. See, his name comes up and I have this ringtone especially for him."

Yeah, I assumed that much since every time Franklin called, her phone began singing "Everything to Me" by Monica. But she shoves the phone in my line of view, and I see his name as clear as day on the screen. "Hmm, that is weird. Have you seen him today?"

"No, not at all. I went by his algebra class but he wasn't there. And he wasn't in lunch."

"So you haven't talked to him all day?" That is strange. Krystal and Franklin are usually together as much as they can be during the school day.

"No. And only once over the weekend. I wonder if he's okay. His father said he was still feeling a little shaky after the accident at the lake on Friday. But that was yesterday morning when I called his house because I wasn't getting an answer on his cell."

We are maybe six feet from the side door, passing the main office and nearing the health suite. Krystal is walking closest to the wall, me only about a foot away from her. The door to the health suite swings open unexpectedly, crashing right into Krystal and just barely missing me.

Krystal drops everything in her arms and hands as she flails backward, hitting the floor with her backside with a loud thump. I'm at her side, immediately pulling the hand away she brought up to her face as she groans.

"Hey, you okay?" I'm asking at the exact moment Alyssa strolls out of the health suite.

"Oh, what happened, Krystal? Did you fall?" she asks in that sickening voice of hers.

I'm helping Krystal sit up, and we both glare at a smiling Alyssa.

"You did that on purpose," Krystal accuses, rubbing her bruised but, thankfully not broken or bloodied, nose.

"Me?" Alyssa feigns innocent. She's a sucky actress, so I'm sure Krystal, just like me, can see through her charade. "I was just coming out of the health suite, minding my own business. How was I supposed to know you were walking down the hall at this precise moment?"

That was a damned good question. Almost as if she were tracking Krystal's movements...but how could she have done that? The cell phone.

"Not funny, Alyssa. And so not cool," I say as I help Krystal with her books and then to stand.

"No, it wasn't," Krystal says taking her stuff back and moving a step closer to Alyssa. "And the next time you want to approach me, be bold enough to do it face-to-face, not using some cheap trick instead."

"Get out of my face. You don't deserve to be this close to our kind," says Alyssa.

Alyssa is running her mouth, but I see the step she takes back when Krystal gets close up on her again.

"Cut it out, Alyssa. She's right—if you have a problem with her, then just address it and get it over with. These games are for children."

Alyssa lifts a brow as she stares at me. "*Underprivileged* children, Sasha. We don't have time for games. We've got more important things to do."

I know what she's talking about and hate that she's saying it in front of Krystal. Being involved with Alyssa in any way is not fun for me, but I know what my parents want from our connection.

"Just chill, Alyssa. We can discuss the other stuff later," I say, then pull Krystal toward the door.

We walk in silence until we get to the car, and I can't help but feel bad. "Sorry about that," I say, like I'm the one who slammed the door into her face.

Krystal just waves a hand. "Alyssa's a bitch, and one of these days I'm not going to be able to hold my temper with her."

"Don't get upset," I say. "We don't know what will happen with our powers if we do. I mean, they're going all wonky now."

"Not wonky, manifesting. I told you that before. I'm seeing even more ghosts, helping them with issues and listening to what they're saying. Some of them lately have been really old, like from another time period. They're warning me all the time. And now these visions." She shakes her head as if trying to get a grasp on things. "We're changing for a reason. We have a purpose."

I nod my head. "I agree. I wonder if because you can see ghosts if you could possibly see on this other plane."

She shrugs. "You think there's an entrance to this plane that we could take without astrally traveling there?"

"There's gotta be. Those creatures can't all have astral projection powers."

"Are you ready to go home?" a nearby voice says.

Both me and Krystal jump and let out little yelps at the sound of Mouse's voice. We didn't hear him approach, and then suddenly here he is. I hope he didn't hear what we were talking about. Then again, I wonder if Mouse hears more than he lets on and what he thinks of it all.

We climb into the car and I don't get to ask him because he turns on the radio and we're forced to listen to Jay-Z. Mouse loves Jay-Z. I don't, and it's my car, but usually I just go ahead and listen to it. My thoughts are drifting beyond the music anyway.

# sixteen

krystal and I came up with nothing yesterday afternoon. Actually, I think the afternoon was hampered by Krystal's preoccupation with where Franklin was and the Alyssa incident. She was at my house for close to an hour before leaving.

That actually turned out to be a good thing since, around a half hour after she left, my mother came home. If I thought my parents were going to flip over me hanging with Antoine, they'd have had just a mild coronary at seeing Krystal. Even though Krystal's stepdad has some money, my parents aren't impressed. Krystal's family doesn't live in Sea Point, so they can't possibly be elite. It's that social class thing again. It makes me sick to even acknowledge that's the way my parents are. I mean, really, not liking someone because they chose a different occupation in life and hence makes less money is totally insane. I wish I could make my parents understand that.

Besides, I'm still grounded, so having company was probably a breach of those rules some kind of way. My mother came to my room to check on me but I just lay in my bed pretending to be asleep. I didn't want to talk to her at all.

This morning, Casietta's in the kitchen, and she's acting kind of strange. I try to ignore it because she gets this way sometimes when she wants to go home to visit her family. But I think today might be different.

Our kitchen is huge, with granite tiled floors and granite counters. All the appliances are stainless steel and built for a kitchen that caters to more than just three people on a daily basis. Well, I guess I should count Mouse and Casietta and Fritz, my dad's driver and the part-time gardener. Still, I think it's too big.

I usually have breakfast sitting at the island while Casietta goes about her morning ritual of scrubbing the already clean counters and taking stock of what's in the always full cabinets. She has my bowl of oatmeal, half grapefruit and glass of milk ready when I come down. I don't want it. That cereal in the back of the cabinet with the fruity marshmallows in it seems much more appealing. But I know Casietta gets her orders regarding my diet straight from my mother.

I eat the grapefruit first because the bittersweet taste buffers the milk that I absolutely do not like. The plan is that by the time I finish the grapefruit and half the glass of milk the oatmeal will be cold. A good excuse not to eat it.

"You be careful at school today," Casietta warns just before slamming another cabinet shut.

"It's just school," I say, scooping up another piece of grapefruit. To mask the tart taste, Casietta uses a packet of sugar substitute. I love Casietta.

"You never know. Danger is all around you. Be careful."

Her voice sounds dire. I look up at her. She's a short, stout woman who gives the best, warmest hugs ever. Her dark hair is just graying around the temples and she keeps it pulled back in a tight bun. Her skin is the same complexion as mine and my mother's, an olive tone that makes us look exotic. Although she's wrinkling a bit at the neck and the creases of her eyes, Casietta looks exactly the same to me that she has forever.

On second glance, I take those words back. Her eyes look

a little darker this morning as she's staring at me so intently. "Mouse will stick closer to the building today. He won't be far from you."

"Why?" I ask, suddenly very concerned with what Casietta isn't saying.

"Because I want you safe."

"I'm usually safe when I'm at school. Casietta, what's going on?"

She stops at another cabinet, her back turned to me. Then, taking a deep breath and releasing it, she picks up a cloth and moves to the sink to wet it. Once the cloth is wet to her specifications, Casietta picks up the bottle of cleaning fluid, sprays it and starts to scrub the counter. The one that's already so clean I could probably apply my makeup by looking into it.

Through all this, she doesn't answer me. I slip from the stool and go over to her, placing a hand on her shoulder. "Is there something wrong, Casietta?"

She turns to me and begins speaking rapid Spanish. Of course, I know the language but can't keep up with her hysterical ranting. By the time she's finished, tears are flooding her eyes and my heart's thumping in my chest.

Then she looks at me, covers her mouth as if she's said something she shouldn't and begins to shake her head. "Be careful. Be careful," she says and drops the cloth before walking hastily out of the kitchen.

I bend to pick up the cloth, her rantings in Spanish running back through my head.

*Luna llena.* Full moon.

*Oscura contra la luz.* Dark versus light.

*Muy pronto.* Coming soon.

Those are the snatches of her conversation I remember.

And they're enough to make me wonder about what Casietta knows and to also make me think I should probably heed her warnings.

Alyssa doesn't meet me at my locker this morning. I'm not upset about that at all. What does worry me is that when I do see Krystal in the hall, instead of her waving or even walking in my direction, she looks me right in the eye, turns and walks away.

I don't have time to follow her and figure out what's going on because the first bell rings. Just before I make it to my class, Antoine grabs my arm.

"Hey, pretty girl."

"Hi," I say a bit breathlessly.

"What are you doing this evening, say around six?"

Uh, being unfairly grounded for yet another day. "Nothing."

"I'll pick you up."

I should say no. I should tell him I'm grounded or make up some other excuse. I should do something other than allow him to come to my house. "Why don't I just meet you someplace?"

He pauses, cocks his head to the side and gives me that half smile he's famous for. "Can you just come to my house?"

Oh no. I can't. I shouldn't. I already know the answer to this question. Why don't I just say it? "Sure. Text me your address."

Then I have to go or risk detention for being late. He kisses me quick on the lips right in front of everybody that's in the hallway. I don't have time to react, I just head into English Lit and take my seat.

Before starting today's lesson, Mrs. Powell says in a real somber voice, "I was told by the principal this morning that we were to make this announcement. We're not making it to fuel any gossip or to start any confusion. We, the administrators, as well as the local authorities, just think it's best that everyone in town know exactly what's going on."

Wow, this seems serious. The whole class is quiet, and she didn't even have to ask them to get that way.

"Another teenager's body was found this morning. This one was behind some office building on Main Street." She clears her throat. "It was in the same condition as the teenager they found last Friday."

And just as she says that, the room gets darker. The sun was out when I stepped out of the car and came into the building. But now it's covered by clouds so dark they almost look black. This makes the classroom dim and solicits a few murmurs from the other kids.

I feel a sense of dread coming over me and start to drum my fingers on the desk. It's an annoying sound. I know because I hated when Krystal kept doing it the other day. Now, I'm doing it and I don't know why.


"It's not a coincidence," Jake says when we're all at the lunch table.

All morning all anybody could talk about was the two boys, the two dead boys found with no eyes. David Sutherby was the first boy. The one we saw at the lake. The one Krystal's ghost identified. And Jack Daily was the second one found last night behind the news station building in town. They were both sixteen years old, both from the Pennsylvania tour bus that was coming from the religious retreat.

"Why would he bother them?" Krystal asks. "Why were they targeted?"

We all sort of agree this has to be connected to the Darkness although we never really say it.

"What else do you know about this retreat they were on?" I ask Lindsey, who so far had the most details about the bodies.

"It was a youth retreat focused on washing away sin, purifying the soul, stuff like that."

"So were they doing some rituals? You know something that may have backfired," Jake asks.

Lindsey looks at him like his words are somehow a curse to her. "What do you mean, like voodoo or witchcraft?" Lindsey asks.

"Like something that would take their eyes out," he replies.

"I think it's some form of punishment," Krystal says.

"Or a message," I add.

Jake frowns. "A message to us? For us?"

I think of Casietta's words this morning and the female voice the first time I ventured to the other plane. "A warning," I whisper.

Our table goes quiet for a minute only to be interrupted by an uninvited guest.

"Well, looks like the gang's all here," Alyssa says with a smirk.

But today she's not alone. Franklin's standing right beside her. Krystal looks confused as she opens her mouth to speak.

"Franklin? Where have you been?" Krystal asks, totally ignoring Alyssa whose arms are crossed over her chest, cherry gloss covered lips upturned at the corners.

"He's been with me," Alyssa answers first.

Krystal rolls her eyes at Alyssa, then looks back at Franklin expecting an answer from him. What she gets is a shrug of his shoulders and a noncommittal, "I've been around."

Franklin looks a little different today. Then again, I haven't seen him since last Friday when Antoine and Jake dragged him out of the lake. Today he's wearing dark-colored jeans, tennis shoes and a tight fitting black T-shirt. That's what's different. Franklin usually wears polo shirts, in all different colors, and his tennis shoes usually match the colors of his shirts. His honey complexion looks a little darker, too, like he's gotten a little sun in the days he's been incommunicado.

Krystal doesn't look too happy with his answer. "Have you gotten my messages?" she asks.

Franklin looks at Alyssa, who throws her head back and laughs. He smiles as he looks back at Krystal. "I lost my phone."

"Yeah, right," Jake mumbles.

"Did you say something, Tracker?" Franklin looks past Krystal and asks Jake.

Jake immediately strikes back. "That's not my name."

"I'm feeling lots of tension here. It's strange," Lindsey is saying from beside me. Her voice isn't that loud, like she's thinking out loud instead of really talking to us.

"They're all jokes," Alyssa says, putting a hand on Franklin's arm.

That's when I notice that Franklin's been holding this carton of milk in his hand the whole time. I'm not sure what's going on. This whole episode is strange, just like Lindsey said. But I think I should do something, say something. But what? Nothing has been directed at me, so maybe I should just keep my mouth out of it.

"Yeah, you're right," Franklin says and begins tossing the carton of milk up and down in his hand. It's not open, so I guess it's no big deal.

Krystal looks crushed at Franklin's words or his weird behavior—which one hurts her most I'm not sure.

"Let's get out of here before the losers rub off on us," Alyssa says.

Then, just when I think we can all breathe a sigh of relief that she's leaving, she looks at me. "You coming, Sasha? I was thinking we could start making some plans for that little project we're working on."

I open my mouth to speak because now I know exactly what Alyssa's trying to do. But it's too late.

Franklin's carton of milk goes up in the air, but his hand neglects to catch it this time. It falls onto the table right in front of Krystal. I could swear the impact isn't that hard, still the carton bursts open, splattering chocolate milk all over Krystal.

Lindsey squeals, and Jake immediately jumps up, a curse already on his lips. Alyssa and Franklin both break out into elaborate fits of laughter.

"See you tonight, Sasha," Alyssa manages to say just a second before the bell rings and she and Franklin walk off arm in arm.

I want to smack her. No, I really wanted to punch Franklin in his stupid weather-boy face. Instead, I find some napkins on the other end of the table and move around to help Krystal clean up.

She's wearing a white shirt today and white capris, so the chocolate milk makes thick brown marks all over her. It's dripping from her hair, sliding in murky rivulets down her cheeks. Lindsey's already helping her and so is Jake. But when I try…

"I don't need your help," she says in a tone she's never used with me before.

I brush it off. "Let's just get to the bathroom and we can use some water to get it out of your hair."

"No!" Krystal yells. "Just..." She hesitates like she wants to say more but then just sighs. "Just get away. Go plan something with her."

"Her" is spoken on a broken whimper. Krystal is trying not to cry. She's embarrassed and hurt over Franklin's betrayal. But why is she taking it out on me?

"I'm only trying to help," I say.

Jake interrupts. "Maybe you should just go, Sasha. We can handle this."

Okay, now it's two against one. I look to Lindsey for some bit of help. She just looks confused, shrugging as she dabs already soaked napkins over Krystal's books.

Fine! I think to myself and drop the napkins I'm holding on the table. If they don't want me around, I won't stay around. It's time to go back to class anyway.

# seventeen

BY five after six I'm a bundle of nerves. I came right home from school still stressed about what happened in the cafeteria.

I can't believe Krystal took that attitude with me. Nor can I believe that Jake, who was actually my friend first, sided with her. I guess it's because he has a crush on her. But then there's Lindsey. Well, I can't really say she took their side. She actually just looked stuck in the middle.

And what was up with Franklin?

It's all just too strange, and the more I try to figure it out, the weirder it seems. So after I sit in my room stewing about that for about an hour, I finally decide to do some homework.

Reading more of the *Iliad* is giving me a better understanding of the Greeks and their beliefs and how parallel their world seems to mine. Like, I know there's always good and evil and governments put into place to secure the safety of the people. The Olympians and the Titans tried to do just that. Only they, the gods I mean, were just as warped and deceitful as the enemies they were supposed to protect the mortals from. Just like our government.

Around six-thirty Casietta comes into my room with a glass of milk. I know it's just her way of checking on me, so I make sure to smile a lot and appear as cheerful as possible until she leaves. She looks at me funny the entire time, and for a split second, just as she's leaving, I think I see something eerie in her eyes. Like a shift in color or shape. Just a subtle change, yet I notice it.

I'm going crazy. I know this. Everything around me is going totally whacky.

The one sane person I know is Antoine. And he's waiting for me to come over to his house.

I know I can't ask Mouse to take me—that'd be just like telling my parents where I'm going. So instead, I boot up my laptop and, sitting cross-legged on my bed, begin to surf the internet for bus routes and schedules in Lincoln. We're a small town, so public transportation information is printed on the town's bare-bones website. After figuring out the route and the bus fare, I change into a jean skirt, a pink lace cami and my matching jean jacket. My hair is still straight from this morning when I'd flat-ironed it, so I only have to run the brush through it a couple of times for it to look decent. A little mascara and a lot of pink gloss and I'm set.

Now to figure out how I'm going to get out of the house.

I have to sneak out, that's simple enough. So as I'm creeping through the hallway, I keep telling myself that this is worth it. Once downstairs, I go straight to the kitchen and to the side door. Punching in the code to the alarm system, I wait impatiently for it to beep, then I open the door and slip out. Casietta's bedroom is on the same floor as mine, but all the way on the other side of the house. Tonight's Tuesday so she's probably already propped up in her bed with a bag of Skittles, watching one of her favorite medical dramas on television.

The air outside is still warm, and I look back and forth down the little path that splits off to wrap around the back of the house toward the gazebo—the place that would now and forever belong to me and Antoine. Heading straight, I cut through Casietta's vegetable garden to get to the line of trees that surround the house. The trees are all more than six feet tall since my father had them installed specifically for privacy. Coming to a stop in front of them, I take a deep breath and focus.

By visualizing where I want to be, I can disappear from one spot and appear in the one I visualized. At least that used to be the way my teleportation worked. But with the other change in my power, I don't know what'll happen this time.

What I do know is that each of my powers revolves around me, what I'm feeling, how I'm able to focus, to become one with the power. I have to open myself up to the power within, embrace it totally, even though I don't know why I have it or really what I'm supposed to be doing with it. So as I stand there, I'm aware of every part of my body in magnification. My arms seem stronger, my hearing more acute, my fingertips tingling. Energy, that's what it feels like, a burst of energy, moving through my veins, down my legs, to my feet that instantly feel like they're lifting off the ground.

Teleportation is quick, not like when I go through that other plane. I stumble just a little as my feet hit solid ground again, and I'm looking at the light post on the corner at the end of the stretch of houses where I live. My house is at the top of that stretch, a good distance from where I am now.

Turning, I walk quickly the next two blocks to the bus stop, and just in time, the bus pulls up. The ride across town isn't long, probably because Lincoln isn't that big. Anyway, I see the sign that says Bolten Street, and I stand up and move toward the door to get off.

Today has been a seasonably warm spring day. But as I take the first couple of steps on the sidewalk, a chilly breeze begins to blow. Strange weather seems to be the norm in Lincoln and never really bothered me before. But now that I know my power's connected to excess energy in weather events, every difference in temperature has me on alert.

Antoine's house, according to the directions I configured between MapQuest and the bus route, should be about two blocks down the street, on the left-hand side. I'm on the right-hand side, so I cross and keep walking. The breeze kind of picks up, blowing my hair around so that I'm probably going to look like a plucked Chihuahua when I get to his house. I lift one hand, trying to smooth it down, but it's useless because the other side just flies up. Groaning in frustration, I step off the curb to cross over to the next block.

My next step is halted when something steps out in front of me. I don't scream immediately because my hair's in my eyes and I can't really see who it is. But then I hear laughter, the same dark, husky laughter I know I've heard before. And I look up. It's him, or it. The Darkness.

Taller than the lamppost on the corner and so wide he's blocking my path. I keep saying *he* because the voice and laughter sound male. But there's no face, no eyes, no nothing, but blackness.

Hearts aren't meant to pump as fast as mine is, so I know that getting away from him is the best possible action to keep my health intact. I try to skirt around him, but he just laughs some more. I back up, but there feels like there's a wall or something behind me, holding me in place. I could scream, but who would hear me? There's a row of houses down the next block, but I'm not sure my voice will travel that far.

I'm trapped.

I hate that feeling. Like I'm helpless to do anything to stop this entity from taunting me, from taunting us. It won't tell us what it wants, and we don't really know how to fight against it. Yet that's exactly what I want to do. Fight.

Rage is building inside me, swirling in thick ugly waves. I've never felt this way before, and my entire body shakes with it. Somewhere in the distance, though, there's this calm trying to take hold of me, trying to get its grasp on me. But how can I stay calm when this thing is so persistent, so insistent on getting to us?

The shaking stops. He's still there. Standing. Waiting. I think he knows what I'm feeling. Probably even what I'm thinking. He's feeding off the rage—I can tell because as long as I'm angry he's not laughing. I'm doing exactly what he wants.

Calm grows, moving inside me until my fingers are tingling again, the sensation touching me everywhere. And just when he starts to say something to me, I teleport.

My feet hit the ground so hard I lose my balance and fall backward. When I should have fallen, Antoine catches me instead.

"Hey, be careful," he says as both his arms hold me, pushing me back upright. "I texted you a while ago. You didn't respond, so I was going to meet you at the bus stop."

"What?" I'm still a little fuzzy after my hasty getaway. Looking around, I see I'm on a small porch.

It's big enough to fit two plastic chairs and one huge plant that looks like it's about to bust right out of the ceramic pot it's planted in. Antoine is standing in front of me. Behind him is a screened door and a window with the yellow glow of light behind it.

"I was coming to meet you," he repeats.

Forcing my mind to get rid of the spooky darkness that keeps following me, I clear my throat. "Um, how did you know I'd be on the bus?"

He just laughs. "I know you weren't having your driver bring you to my house. Come on inside."

I follow him through the screened door and into the warm house. I do not respond to his comment because that will just start a conversation I don't want to have right now.

Antoine's house reminds me of Jake's, even though Jake lives east, toward the creek and the railroad tracks. But the house is narrow and long like Jake's. It's warm like Jake's, too, and I wonder if one of Antoine's grandparents lives here.

"We can sit here and watch television," Antoine says, pointing to a couch that looks like it's seen a lot of years.

That's not a bad thing, I think as I sit down, because it's really comfortable. The white couch in our living room, the one we've had for about three years, I think, I've sat in that one maybe two times. It's hard, not welcoming at all. But this one is. It's a dark brown color, with like a corduroy feel to it. There are red pillows on each end. Across the room is an entertainment stand with a bunch of pictures and knickknacks on it. It also holds the TV, nineteen inch, I believe. There's a VCR and a DVD player on top of it and a small library of movies on the two shelves beneath it.

"You want something to drink?" Antoine asks.

He doesn't sit down with me, just sort of stands in front of me looking more than a little nervous.

"No. Thanks," I say rubbing my hands down my thighs. I'm a little nervous, too. And I'm still shaky from teleporting twice in the last hour.

"Wanna watch a movie?" he asks, taking a seat beside me.

I shrug. "I can't stay long."

He nods while picking up the remote control. "I figured that."

Again there's that tone, like there's something else he wants to say. Or maybe it's a preamble to a conversation we've sort of had before that I want to steer clear of. So I just ignore it and stare at the screen.

Halfway through the movie, *Bad Boys II*, Antoine's pick but one I've seen before and enjoyed, a woman comes into the room. She's carrying a small tray with two glasses and two saucers with slices of cake on them.

"Thanks, Aunt Pearl," Antoine says and immediately stands up to help the woman with the tray.

I slide to the edge of the couch and nervously smile at her. The smile she gives me in return is warm and genuine, her high cheekbones lifting even higher. She's about my height, I guess, with dark brown skin and dark eyes. Her hair is up in some sort of twist, black, no signs of gray.

"This is Sasha. Sasha, this is my aunt Pearl." Antoine makes the introductions.

I figure I should stand, extend my hand, open my mouth and say something. Wow, I'm acting like such a goof.

"Ah, hi. It's nice to meet you."

She takes my hand, shakes it heartily. "It's nice to finally meet you, Sasha. You can call me Aunt Pearl, too. That's what everybody calls me."

The nervous jitters I was feeling sort of melt beneath her gaze and her words. She's looking at me like she's really happy to meet me.

"Okay, Aunt Pearl."

"You like cake?"

Does a cow make milk? "Yes, ma'am." My mother would have a fit if she saw me. But she's not here, so I sit back down and take the plate Antoine's offering to me.

"Aunt Pearl makes the best red velvet cake in the world," he says, foregoing the fork on the platter and picking his cake up before taking a huge bite out of it.

I take my fork, even though I'm really tempted to follow

Antoine's lead. Cutting a reasonably sized piece, I put it in my mouth and chew. It's sooooo good. I smile. "It's the best I've ever tasted."

I hope that doesn't sound phony, because I'm being really honest. The cake is moist and the icing's sweet. And for a moment I feel like I'm at home. In a real home, with real people who actually talk to each other and love each other. Not like the chilly atmosphere in the fortress I live in.

For the rest of the movie, Aunt Pearl joins us, laughing at Will Smith and Martin Lawrence as if this is the first time she's seen this movie—although she told me she's watched it several times before. When the credits begin to roll, I notice its almost ten o'clock.

"I have to go," I say to Antoine.

"She's right," Aunt Pearl says. "It's a school night. Don't keep her out too late. Take her home, Antoine."

While he's taking the DVD out of the machine and turning everything off, Aunt Pearl comes over to me as I stand up.

"Don't be a stranger now, Sasha. You come back and visit me real soon."

"I sure will," I say, meaning every word. "I really had a good time tonight."

"Well, I'm glad. But the next time I'll cook you a meal. Get some meat on your bones." She chuckles and tweaks my chin.

I smile just as Antoine comes up and takes my hand. "Let's get you home."

The ride back to my house is quiet. I'm thinking of all the things I've been thinking since first meeting Antoine. We have such different backgrounds, and yet, I really like him.

Getting out of the car after he parks at the end of my street instead of in the driveway, we walk in silence until we arrive at the gazebo. It's risky, I know, since I'm not technically supposed to be outside, but we sit down right next to each other.

"You still act like you're scared that we're together," Antoine says.

I shrug. "We're just different," I say in a voice real hushlike since I'm sneaking around out here.

He turns my face to his and takes my hand in his. Our foreheads rest together. His touch warms me, his presence completes me. This whole thing between us is confusing, but I think the answer is becoming clearer.

"You're a girl and I'm a boy," he says, and his voice is hushed, too.

It's like we're in our own private world, right here, sitting in the center of my, no, *our* gazebo.

"You know what I mean."

He shakes his head, just a little, not enough to break our contact. "I know what I want."

"I know what I want, too. But—"

"No 'buts'," he says quickly, and then he tilts his head so that his lips can easily touch mine.

I absolutely love kissing him. His lips are so soft, but he always seems to be in control. I really want to be with him. He said that's all that matters. I'm wondering if that's true.

My parents would freak if they found out I was seeing Antoine. The cause of that freak-out would be for so many reasons: (1) he's definitely not a Richie; (2) his brother was the one murdered by the pervert molester teacher a few months back, which was just too much scandal for the Carringtons to handle; and finally (3) he's black. I don't think my parents are racially prejudiced—just tied up in that social thing—but I think they'd prefer me with a white boy, again to cut down on scandal. Image, after all, like my mother's mantra, is everything. But feelings should account for something. Especially the ones swirling through me right now. It's warm and giddy-like, reminds me of when I was a kid getting up on Christmas morning and seeing all my gifts. But ten times better.

His hands move on my arms, down until he's grabbing my waist. Momentarily baffled, I stop concentrating on the kiss, but then he just lifts me up until I'm sitting in his lap. Who knew he was that strong?

I lock my ankles behind his back and hope I'm not blushing since this is the most intimate position I've ever been in with a boy.

"I really like you, Sasha."

"I really like you, too." And I hope this is for real. I mean, I hope he's not playing me or anything because my "like" might just be moving in another direction.

His arms around my waist are holding me tight, mine are around his neck. I'm trying not to choke him, but I don't want to let go. The kiss is deeper when he opens his mouth. My heart's about to pitter-patter right out of my chest, so I hold on even tighter.

If this is a dream, I don't want to wake up.

If this is heaven, death isn't so bad.

But if this is fake and heartache is just around the corner… well, let's just not even go there.

# eighteen

Things that make me Sasha Carrington:

1. My parents are rich—well, not like Donald Trump rich, but by Lincoln, Connecticut, standards they're like maybe movie-star rich.
2. I live in a huge house in the elite neighborhood called Sea Point.
3. I drive a BMW—actually, Mouse drives it, but next year it'll be all mine!
4. My weekly allowance probably looks like an adult McDonald's worker's two-week paycheck.

Things that make me a Mystyx:

1. I can teleport.
2. I can now astral project.
3. I have the birthmark that I think comes from the powers of the River Styx.

Things that just make me…me:

1. I love cheeseburgers.
2. I consider red fingernail polish a huge fashion mistake and I don't care who disagrees.

3. When I grow up I want to be an astronaut.
4. I'm in love with Antoine Watson.

Lists are like one of my other hobbies. I do it to keep myself organized, so that I don't get all twisted up with stuff in my mind and go crazy. I've seen so many people go crazy. Well, not exactly firsthand, but reality television's a curse and a blessing. I could probably lock myself in the house for the next five years watching only reality shows and grow up just as opinionated, obnoxious and emotionally disturbed as most of the kids at Settleman's High will become.

So today's lists are just to remind me that I'm juggling a lot of personality. All the different aspects of me are both intriguing and troublesome. Yet I don't think I can change any of them. I am what I am.

That sounds so philosophic. But I'm convinced it's true.

Riding to school, I keep thinking about my list, about how Sasha Carrington has morphed into a Mystyx. I like the power I have. I like the friends it has brought me: Jake, Krystal and even Lindsey. I'd really like to find out how we're supposed to fight this Darkness so we can kick his evil dark butt and get on with our lives.

But, apparently, that'll have to wait until after first period because the warning bell rings just as I get to school.

I hurry up to class, seeing Alyssa out of the corner of my eye and ducking into a crowd of kids so she doesn't see me. I'm still ticked at her for what she did to Krystal yesterday and not at all sure how she got her claws into Franklin. So I definitely do not want to see her right now.

I would have liked to see Krystal, to make sure she is okay today, but I don't have that kind of luck. I get into the classroom just as the late bell rings and fall into my seat, not quite ready to start my learning day, but as close as I'm going to get.

Today must be my day to run late. It's been lunchtime for fifteen minutes, but I'm just walking into the cafeteria. Mr. Emory stopped me for a report on the field trip last week, as if he wasn't there and didn't see the repulsive dead body come to surface for himself. So I spent valuable time talking to him when I should have been at the table checking on Krystal and telling the other Mystyx what I've learned.

When I get to the table, everybody shuts up. I mean, I think I actually hear the click of teeth as their mouths close so quickly, so completely.

"Hey," I say airily. "What's going on?"

"Nothing," Krystal snaps and looks away from me.

"Hi, Sasha," Lindsey says, giving me a small smile. I notice she's wearing a black blouse today. She can't read any thoughts. That's probably for the best since I don't think my thoughts are particularly nice at the moment.

"Jake, you okay?" I ask because his face is all red and he's clenching his fists.

"Fine. I'm just fine."

"You sure? You don't look fine."

"Oh come on. What do you want him to say? How do you think he is after what your family's doing to his?" Krystal thrusts these words at me with the force of a virtual slap to my face. I'm getting kind of tired of her attitude, especially since I haven't done anything to deserve it.

"My family? What do they have to do with anything?"

Jake refuses to answer.

I reach out and touch his arm, but he pulls away from me.

Now I'm getting angry. "If you have something to say, Jake, just say it."

For a few seconds it's quiet—well, as quiet as it's going to get in a room full of teenagers.

"You don't have to have everything!" The words burst from his mouth. His lips tighten and he continues, "There's nothing wrong with our house. I know it's not as big and pretty as yours but we like it. It's ours. My dad worked hard to pay for it. And your father has no right to it!"

WTH? I'm trying to follow his words and cut through the tension boiling at our table. Krystal's looking at me like she's really contemplating hitting me. Lindsey's rocking back and forth, her forehead pinched like she's in pain. Jake's fists are planted on the table, but I know if he lifts them, if he directs the rage apparently boiling inside him, it's not going to be good.

So I level my voice and look straight into his eyes. "I don't know what you're talking about, Jake. Did my father say something to your father? Tell me what happened. Maybe I can help."

"You can't help. He's Marvin Carrington, the all-powerful in Lincoln. He wants something, he just takes it. Just like that. He wants to build some exclusive club on our property, so we have to go. My house gone! My family homeless! He doesn't give a damn!"

With that, Jake jumps up, his nostrils flaring as he glares at me. "I'm outta here," he finally says before stomping off.

Krystal goes after him, leaving me to sit dumbfounded at the table.

I know about my dad's plan for the club. I think the premise of it is stupid, but I reluctantly agreed to help him. I had no idea he was planning to build the club on the property where Jake's house is. I would have tried to stop him. Wouldn't I?

★ ★ ★

The afternoon ticks by slowly, my thoughts completely on getting home so I can talk to my dad. Why would he want to tear down Jake's house just to build the club? Probably because Jake lives by Dent Creek, the poorest section of Lincoln. If I know my dad, he most likely thinks he's doing a good thing by knocking down those houses. He wouldn't think about the people who live there, the families.

But I'm thinking about them. I'm thinking about Jake and his grandfather, who told us about our power, and his father, who I rarely ever see but I know he's there. Where will they go if they have to leave their homes?

I'm thinking about this so hard my head starts to hurt. The final bell rings for the day, and I'm so relieved I just about bolt up out of my seat.

I walk through the halls in a daze, not really seeing or hearing anyone or anything around me. Grabbing my stuff out of my locker is a repetitive action. I do it and don't even realize I'm done until I'm heading back down the hall toward the front door. Earlier I thought about trying to stop Jake after school to talk to him again, but I figure it's pointless. He's angry right now. Best I wait until I have all the facts and possibly a solution before I approach him again.

I have one goal right now and that's to get home and talk to my dad. I want to know what's going on with Jake's house and if there's any way he can build someplace else.

Forces beyond my control obviously have another plan.

Just before I get to the front door, I see Franklin and Alyssa. The sight of them together again has my head throbbing more. They're up to something. I don't know how I know, I just do.

So I turn and walk toward them. As I get closer, I hear them laughing and see that Alyssa's holding something in her hand.

"What's up?" I say the minute I approach them.

They both look at each other, then back at me and laugh again. Whatever they think is so funny I'm thinking has got to be bad.

"What's up with you?" Franklin says, and his eyes are doing this weird thing.

I've heard the saying *eyes dancing* before, but never actually took it literally. Well, Franklin's are. They're moving around really fast, and the color is changing. Normally his eyes are brown, I think. I don't really stare at his eyes a lot. But this golden color that I'm seeing is definitely not normal.

I open my mouth to say something, but before I can, they stop. Now they're still and they're brown.

He's still smiling at me, wearing black jeans and a black shirt. Similar to what he wore yesterday.

"Nothing. Just wondering why you two are together again. Where's Krystal, Franklin?" I ask him pointedly.

This just makes both of them laugh more. Alyssa speaks up this time.

"Oh, she's stuck in gym," she says, raising her dark eyebrows up and down and looking at Franklin.

"Yeah, stuck," he echoes.

Yeah, looney, that's what I'm thinking about these two. But then my gaze falls down to what Alyssa's holding in her hand.

"What's that?" I ask.

"Nothing," she answers quickly.

Franklin answers at the same time. "Clothes."

I look back and forth between them, then take a quick step forward and grab Alyssa's arm, lifting it toward me so I can see what's in her hand.

Franklin is right, it's clothes.

Black stretch pants and a light blue top. The top has tiny

rhinestones going around the neckline, and I know I've seen it somewhere before.

"These aren't yours," I say, actually testing the theory circulating in my mind.

"Oh please, you know I don't buy off-the-rack." She acts all indignant but I don't care. I'm thinking about who these clothes might belong to.

"Where did you say Krystal is?"

Franklin sighs. "Stuck. Can't you hear, Carrington?"

Then I feel sick to my stomach. "These are hers, aren't they?"

Alyssa yanks her arm from my grasp and puts a hand on her hip. "Now would your little friend be silly enough to run around the school without her clothes on?"

"No," I say, eyeing them slowly. "But you two would be ignorant enough to take them from her while she's in the locker room changing."

Without waiting for a response or verification from either of them, I turn and run down the hallway toward the gym. Pulling open the double doors, I look all around for Krystal. When I don't see her, I run down the back stairs that lead to the locker rooms, taking them two at a time. The boys' locker room is down the left side of the hallway and the girls down the right. I take off in that direction. Slamming to a stop at the door, I pull and it opens. As soon as I step in, I start calling Krystal's name.

I get no response.

Walking through every aisle of lockers, I just keep calling her. Then I check the showers and still don't see her. It's just as I'm about to give up and leave the locker room that I hear a familiar voice.

"Be vigilant," it says.

It's not Krystal, but the female voice I heard when I was on that other plane.

So I stop, realizing that Krystal has to be somewhere close. On my right side, the *M* is starting to tingle and burn against my skin. I haven't felt this since we all used our powers together to stop Mr. Lyle. Yes, Krystal is definitely close. I can feel it.

Letting the feeling of her closeness guide me, I move through the locker room again until I see the door to the towel closet. I still don't hurry, even though I want to get her out of there immediately. Instead, almost as if following some unwritten instructions, I take my time. With each step, I'm acutely aware of the heat emanating through my *M* more persistently.

When I'm right up on the door, I reach for the handle, but it won't turn. It's locked.

I curse and try to turn it again.

Nothing.

Where's the key? I'm thinking this but have no clue where to look. I've never seen this door locked before. It's always open, with towels neatly stacked or thrown at the floor beside it. But not today.

I have no idea where the key can be. Maybe in the office. The physical education office or the main office? I don't know which one, and I don't know how long they've had her locked in here. Krystal hasn't said a word, hasn't muttered a sound in answer to my repeated calling of her name. But I know she's in there.

And that knowledge holds me still. It keeps me from running, screaming for help. I just focus on Krystal. Wondering if she's afraid, if she's all right. I can visualize holding the key in my hand and opening up the door.

The key.

To open the door, I need the key.

Where is the key?

My feet hit the floor and I open my eyes. I'm standing in the middle of the physical education office. Without another thought, I go right to the top desk drawer, pull it open and retrieve the large ring of keys.

It takes me another second or so to think about Krystal in that closet, and then I'm there, too. Putting the key into the lock, I turn it, then use my other hand to turn the knob and open the door.

"Are you okay?" I ask her even though I know she's not.

Her chest is moving up and down rapidly as if she'd been the one running to get here. Her eyes are furious as she takes a step toward me.

While I know she's angry, I don't step back because why would she be angry with me? I'm the one who got the key and let her out.

"How did they do this to you? Why did they do this?" I'm asking her these questions even though I don't really think she'll answer.

"Get away from me," she says.

Now I didn't expect that.

"I just helped you out," I say in defense as she pushes past me.

"But you're the one who started all this in the first place."

She doesn't turn back to look at me, just keeps on walking away, heading out of the locker room.

"Wait a minute," I yell. "How can you say I started this?"

"You and your rich friend!" she spits as she's pushing through the door.

I follow, being quick to hold my hands out for the swinging

door or else it would have knocked me down. "What? Wait a minute." She doesn't stop walking, but I do. "The least you can do is stop and give me an explanation for what you're accusing me of."

She does stop then, and she comes back to stand in front of me. "The least I can do? Is that what you said? The least you could do is stop fronting and be honest about how you feel. If you don't like me, then just say so and be gone. I don't have time for these petty games. And I certainly don't have time for you smiling in my face one minute and planning my embarrassment the next."

I shake my head from side to side, trying to figure out what she's talking about. "I never said I didn't like you. You know we have a bond that goes way beyond liking each other. It goes beyond this school and these students. How can you stand there and accuse me of trying to embarrass you?"

"This isn't about the Mystyx. It's about you and me. You being a Richie and me being, whatever everybody thinks I am. You never wanted me and Franklin together and now you've got your wish. He's with Alyssa. He's with one of you."

Her words hurt. As much as I want to dismiss her and her crappy attitude, her accusations are painful. Even if they aren't true. "I'm not one of them," I say quietly, and for the first time in my life, for the first time since I heard about this club and what my father was trying to do, the first time since I doubted whether or not I should go out with Antoine, I know those words are absolutely true.

I am not one of them.

I am Sasha Carrington, a fifteen-year-old sophomore at Settleman's High. I am a Mystyx.

I am not a Richie.

I am not one of them.

"Yeah, well, I can't tell," Krystal says. "Look, just stay away from me, okay? I understand we have Mystyx business to handle and I'm not running away from my powers. But other than that, just stay out of my life."

The last she says quietly, and for a second I think it hurts her to say it just as much as it hurts me to hear.

She turns and walks away.

I don't try to stop her this time.

This time, I walk away, too.

# nineteen

I slam the front door behind me, just like I'd slammed the car door when I got out. Mouse hadn't said a word, but I'm almost positive someone in the house will.

I'm wrong.

There seems to be nobody around.

Or nobody in plain sight. I don't even bother going into the kitchen to look for Casietta or upstairs to see if my mother's home. They're not who I want to see.

I head straight down the foyer, past the living room and den and library. At the far end of the house is where my father's office is. I march right up to his door and almost barge right in. Then I decide to knock.

But I hear voices and change my mind about that, too.

My father is not alone.

There's a man in the office with him. I can only hear the two voices but not completely. If I put my ear to the door I'll be able to hear better. I don't even consider it another minute, just lean over and do it.

"We can benefit each other, Marvin. If you put funding into my project, I'll publicly endorse your club," the first male voice says.

"Your project, what's it called again?" That's my dad.

The other man chuckles. "Let's just call it Project S for now."

"What's it about? What are you trying to do with it?"

"I'll just tell you that it's big, Marvin. When I finish with this research, the stuff I'm going to unveil to the world will be staggering."

"Staggering? That's a tall order to fill. We're not talking terrorism or anything, are we? Because I'm not in for that type of attention. I'm just trying to make my mark on Lincoln."

The man laughs again. "You're trying to make Lincoln yours and yours alone. I know what you're planning, Marvin. And I'm not against it. But I've got goals of my own. Goals that Carrington money can help me reach."

"Because the television station isn't paying you enough to reach the goal, is that it?"

"That's it exactly."

I can hear some movement. Somebody's walking around the room.

"This project isn't going to hurt anyone, is it?" My dad asks.

"Only those who have the power to let it hurt them."

At that moment, my side begins to warm again. I pull up my shirt and glance down. My *M* is glowing. Pink, just like before. But why now?

Wait a minute, did my dad just say something about the television station? Walter Bryant? Is that who's in my dad's office talking to him? And he's talking about a project. A project that will only hurt those who have the power to let it hurt them.

The Power.

Those who have the power.

Oh, this is so not good. I've got to tell someone. I've got to tell the Mystyx.

I'm halfway down my driveway when my cell phone rings. Reaching into my back pocket where I stuck it after leaving my purse in the house, I answer.

"Hello?"

"Hey, pretty girl. What're you doing?"

It's Antoine. And he's like the last person I need to talk to right now.

"Ah, nothing. I mean, I can't talk right now."

"Cool," he continues. "I was thinking we could hook up in like an hour or something. Maybe see a movie or just hang out?"

I'm walking while I'm talking, trying to figure out a way to get Antoine off this phone so I can move faster to get to the Mystyx. "Um, no. I can't."

Antoine grows silent on the other end. "You can't or you don't want to?"

I sigh and stop walking. "I can't right now. I've got other plans."

"Yeah, I'll just bet you do. Look, Sasha, I've had enough of this sneaking around. I asked you before if you wanted to be with me and you said you did. But now you're acting all scared again."

I roll my eyes, but that's futile since he's not here to see me. "No, Antoine, it's not like that. I've just got something else to do."

"Okay. What?"

I hesitate. I can't tell him that I have to find my friends so we can find out what Walter Bryant's researching. And I definitely can't tell him that I'm deathly afraid that what Mr. Bryant's researching is me, or my kind.

"Now is just not a good time, Antoine."

"Right. Well, I don't guess any time is ever going to be good for you."

"Wait—" I start to say, but he's already disconnected.

Sticking my phone back into my pocket, I vow to deal with

him later. Now I've got to figure out who to go to first and get there as fast as I can.

I can't go to Krystal.

She's so mad at me, she's not going to listen to a word I say, even though I don't understand how I manage to be the bad guy in this scenario. But I'd just rather not go there with her right now. Besides, this is about Franklin's dad and possibly Franklin, now that I really think about it. He has been hanging with Alyssa all of a sudden. Another reason why Krystal is definitely not the one to go to with this information.

I'm not calling Lindsey.

She's still new to the group, and I'm not real sure where her head is with all this stuff. I mean, she seems like she's down for what we are and what we may have to do. Other than that, I just don't know anything about her. Like, she wasn't in Lincoln last year or even last month for that matter. But she's here now. Just as all this creepy mess has started, Lindsey arrives. And she lives with old Mrs. Hampton who has that big house almost near the end of the town line. I've wondered more than once what's their relation or what's it like living in that big old house. Once upon a time, I thought it was haunted.

Now I know the entire town is probably what's haunted.

So I end up at Jake's.

Kind of figured all along this is where I'd come. I've known Jake the longest. We have a history, so to speak. Ever since the first day of elementary school, I've seen Jake Monday through Friday and sometimes on weekends, depending on where we both were in town. But it wasn't until last summer that we both noticed our connection was deeper than just classmates.

Lifting my arm to knock on his door seems like a ritual. I've done it so many times I don't even realize it now as I wait for someone to come and open it.

"It's you," an old gravelly voice speaks the minute the door is cracked open.

"Hi, Mr. Kramer," I say to Jake's grandfather with a smile on my face. I like him a lot, even though he forgets who I am all the time.

"Thought you'd be coming around soon. Haven't seen you for a while. But I told Jakey, she'll be coming, you watch and see."

He was talking and looking at me strangely with his gray eyes deep set into a face that was far more wrinkly than I think it should be. Mr. Kramer—or Pop Pop as Jake calls him—isn't wearing his glasses today. Well, he's not wearing them where they should be. On top of his mostly bald head, positioned in a lopsided way, are his black rimmed glasses. Still, the way he's looking at me says he can see just fine.

"Ah, can I come in? Is Jake at home?"

"He's here. Mad as a pit bull he is, too," Mr. Kramer says but doesn't budge from the door.

So I take a step forward, hoping this will serve as a sign that I want to come in.

"Pushy today, aren't you," he says with a slow grin spreading across his leathery skinned face. "That power's growing mighty strong. I knew it would. I told them they couldn't hold it back. Fools they are for thinking they could. Big, dumb-assed fools."

Who is he talking about?

Mr. Kramer's always talking, but only half of what he says makes sense and that's only half the time he's talking. I don't know, but I think he's making sense now.

"Who did you tell?" I ask, but then the door opens wider and Jake appears right next to his grandfather.

"You shouldn't be here," he says, his face still set with that angry glare.

I really hate seeing Jake like this. It looks almost as if he's in pain. I want to make it better, but I don't know how. "Hi," I say quietly. "Can we talk?"

He really doesn't look like he wants to agree.

"You need to be doing more than talking," Mr. Kramer interrupts. "Acting is what's needed. This has been coming for a long time. It's been waiting to make its move. Now's the time."

"Go back inside, Pop Pop," Jake says.

"How do you know?" I ask.

"William told me," he says, then scratches his head like he's trying to think of the next words to say. "He told me it was coming and that only you…your kind…can stop it. Says it's a curse from hell coming back for revenge." Mr. Kramer is quiet for a second, then his fingers grasp his glasses, and he pulls them down from his head. "There they are. Been looking for these for two days now. Can't see *Jeopardy* without 'em."

And just like that, he's gone. Turning his back to me and walking away.

"Something's happened," I say before Jake has a chance to shut the door in my face. I was hoping he wouldn't do that anyway, but right about now I'm not so sure about what Jake will or will not do.

He looks torn, like he really wants to walk away, and then he really wants to stay.

Finally he sighs, steps outside and closes the door behind him.

"What happened?"

"I overheard Franklin's dad talking to my dad."

He sits on the first step and looks back at me with a smirk. "About what, knocking down somebody else's home to build a weather museum?"

I take a seat next to him, carefully considering whether or not to smack him in the back of his head for being so smart.

"No, about this project Mr. Bryant's working on. A project that focuses on strange weather patterns and the excess energy they produce."

Jake is quiet. I knew he would be.

"What do you think this means?"

I shrug, but he's not looking at me, so I say, "I don't know."

We sit in silence.

"A curse from hell doesn't exactly equate to our weather-related powers," he says finally.

"No. But that voice warned me of a curse that she made. I've gotta figure 'she' was Styx, the goddess also known as the river. She was very powerful and she had a direct link to the Underworld."

"Are you hearing yourself, Sasha? You're talking about Greek goddesses and the Underworld, of all things. This is the twenty-first century. There are no gods and goddesses or Underworlds, for that matter."

"There's heaven and hell," I say, as if he should have already known this answer. "Good and bad. Light and dark. No matter what time frame you put us in, there's always been the same battle, the same basic issues to fight over."

He leans back, resting his elbows on the concrete. His head falls back, and his scraggly hair shifts to the side. I have a clear view of his face, which isn't normal. I notice that Jake's a really nice looking guy. His dark brown eyes and wild brown hair give him a boyish cuteness. But the stern set of his chin and his tall, lean stature make him an attractive young man. Funny how I never really saw that before. He's always been just Jake. I wonder if Krystal has noticed.

"Control," he says. "That's a basic issue. One side always wants complete control."

"The bad, evil. The Darkness."

He nods. "But how does Franklin's dad figure into this?"

So I tell Jake what I've been noticing about Franklin and watch again as his face fills with rage. I touch a hand to his thigh this time because, man, I swear he looks like a volcano about to erupt.

"Jake, come on, you've got to get a hold on this."

His fists clench at his sides. "I can't. I mean, I'm trying. It's not like your power, Sasha. Yours or Krystal's. You both seem to have this passive power, this mentally rooted power that flows so seamlessly. Mine is so volatile. I don't know what I'm capable of."

"Like your great-uncle William," I say, still rubbing my hand up and down Jake's leg, noticing that with that action his face seems to loosen up, the tension ebbing slowly away from his body.

"I guess. He didn't know how to handle it either. That's why he ran away. I wish I knew where he was so I could ask him some questions."

"He probably wouldn't have the answers for you. I think we're in charge of our own powers, even if someone before us had them, too. I think our powers are linked to us," I say and use my other hand to tap on my chest. "To who we are and how we're made up. Only we can control our power, Jake. Through our emotions, our thoughts, our actions. We have full control over what we do with our powers. I think that's what makes us so dangerous to the Darkness. That's why he's coming after us."

Jake takes a moment to think on what I've said. Then he sits straight up, looking at me seriously.

"What if Franklin's possessed by the Darkness, the same way Mr. Lyle was? What if that evil is now inside Franklin?"

Following his line of thought, I say, "And what if Franklin's father knows? If he knows about the Darkness, the weather patterns, the excess energy...then he knows about us. He knows about the Mystyx."

"Probably not who we are exactly, but definitely that we exist," Jake offers. "We've got to find out more about this project he's working on," he says, standing up.

"There's only one way to do that," I say. "We've got to get into his office to look at his files."

Jake nods grimly, then we both take the steps and head east toward Main Street where Walter Bryant's office is located.

# twenty

It's after six by the time we get to the office building. It's right across the street from the television station, so there are still some trucks and cameramen standing outside. In the building where the offices are, there's no one, so Jake and I walk right through the glass doors. There's a security guard at the desk.

We stop and look at each other. I don't know what to do or say. For a minute, Jake doesn't seem to either. Then he whispers, "I'll handle it. Just be ready to head for the elevators."

There's a sign as soon as you come through the doors that lists all the offices in this building and the floor numbers. I already spied that Walter Bryant's office is on the third floor. Sticking my hands in my pocket, I try to look casual as Jake walks toward the security guard.

Then I hear something fall and glass breaking. It's the huge frame that holds the picture of Lincoln's mayor. It was hung along the opposite wall from where the office directory is. Now it's on the floor in a heap of broken glass. The security guard swears and heads right over in that direction.

Jake turns to me and, with a nod, says we should head for the elevators. We do, and once inside I touch his arm. "See, you're learning how to use your powers."

He just sighs. "It's not easy."

"Tell me about it," I chime in just as the door opens to the third floor.

The carpet is this dark red color and is worn in some spots and just plain dirty in others. The hall seems to go only one way as the other end is just marked by a door and the bright green Exit sign. There are several offices on this floor, and luckily for us, they all have names on them. So we walk until we see Mr. Bryant's. I quickly grab for the knob and turn.

"Locked," Jake says sullenly.

I nod. "Should have figured that."

"Move back," he instructs.

I don't ask, just do as he says and step aside.

Jake's looking at the knob, he's concentrating, but it's hard to tell that's what he's doing. His face seems the same and so does his stance. I just notice the way his fingers are clenching and releasing at his sides. A clicking sound echoes in the hallway, and I watch in awe as the knob turns and the door opens while neither of us touch it.

I guess any other kid would think these things—our powers—were cool. I'm starting to believe they're just necessary.

I step inside first, with Jake coming in afterwards and closing the door. We go in separate directions looking around the office.

"What are we looking for?" Jake asks finally.

"I don't know. Anything that looks like it relates to a project about the weather."

"He's a weatherman, Sasha. Everything in here is going to relate to the weather."

I am already behind his desk, lifting up papers and folders. "Don't be so logical all the time," I snap. "Just look at stuff. Look in those file cabinets over there."

I hear the cabinets open and know Jake is doing what I say, even as I start opening the desk drawers. The search seems to go on for hours, but I know it's only been a few minutes. Frustrated, I turn away from the desk and lean on it a little too hard. Pictures fall over. As I'm picking them up, I notice one is of Franklin. Looks like a school photo of when he was normal. I mean, he's wearing the clothes I'm used to seeing him in—khaki pants and polo shirts. He's smiling at the camera like he's happy the man behind it is asking him to say cheese. The other photo is of Franklin and his father. Mr. Bryant and Franklin look a lot alike, except for Mr. Bryant's mustache. As I put them both next to each other, I think they both look normal. The same, I guess, as I do on my pictures. But I'm not normal. And something tells me neither are the Bryants.

"Got it!" Jake yells.

I abandon the pictures and walk across the office to where Jake has his hands in one of the file cabinets. He pulls out a folder and flips it so I can see the writing on the front.

"Project S," I read. "That's what he mentioned to my dad."

"Let's find out." Jake opens the folder, and the first thing we see are what looks like reports.

"Majestic 12?" I read on one of the pages.

"Ever heard of that?" Jake asks.

I'm shaking my head. "I don't know. I think it should sound familiar but I'm not sure."

So we flip through some other pages. Photocopies of news articles. A tornado that hit Topeka, Kansas, in 1966. In 1992 a brush fire that ravaged the forests in California. Reported UFO sightings.

"Weather stuff," Jake comments and flips through to the last page in the folder.

We both pause. There in the back of the folder, taped down,

is a plastic bag. Inside the bag is a secure flash drive that can't be downloaded without being detected.

We look at each other and know what we want to do.

"Let's just take it," I say.

Jake is immediately shaking his head in the negative.

"No. He'll notice it's gone. We have to make a copy and replace it."

"Well, I don't know about you but I don't usually run around town with a flash drive in my pocket."

"Okay, you're right. We've gotta come back then."

"You mean leave it?"

"Yeah. We can't let him know we know about this. So we'll leave, go get another flash drive and come back and replace it."

I'm biting on my lower lip, wondering at the logic of what Jake's saying. I know he's right, but really, I want to take that flash drive now. I want to know what's on it, what Mr. Bryant is planning.

"Fine," I say finally, as if my word makes it so. When actually, Jake had already closed up the file and was slipping it back into the cabinet as I spoke.

"Let's get the others and tell them what's going on," he's saying as we head to the door.

He looks around and nods for me to do the same. "Make sure nothing looks disturbed."

I do and ask at the same time, "The others, as in Krystal and Lindsey?"

"You got any others in mind?" he says in his usual dry tone as he heads to the door.

We're back in the hallway now, the door closing as Jake gives the knob another stare that pushes the lock back into place.

"No, it's just that Krystal isn't too happy with me at the moment."

I stop at the elevator, but Jake pulls me along to the door marked Exit. "Yeah, I heard."

After he pushes me through the door, I stop. "It's not my fault. I had nothing to do with what Alyssa and Franklin did to her."

Jake's lips draw into a tight line. "She's hurt over that idiot Franklin. Alyssa just pisses her off and I think she'd just as soon beat her ass than take any more crap from her. But Franklin's really got her trippin'."

I nod and sigh. "I know. I wish I could tell her he's not worth it but she won't even talk to me."

Jake is already taking the steps. "I've tried to tell her but she doesn't want to hear it. But yeah, you're not on our favorites list right about now."

About one flight down I stop and stomp my feet on the steps. "That is not my fault either. As a matter of fact, I was going to talk to my dad about your house when I overheard him talking to Mr. Bryant."

He stops and turns to me. "You were?"

"Yes, I was." I fold my arms across my chest. "You're my best friend, Jake. I don't want you to be shipped out of Lincoln, tossed out of your family home because my dad can't find another piece of land to build on. I'm going to stop him," I say confidently, even though I haven't even talked to my dad about it yet.

So I don't know what Jake's thinking, but for a minute I wish I had Lindsey's mind-reading power. He's just looking at me, and then he's looking at the floor, and then he finally says something. "Let's get out of here."

Not exactly what I was expecting, but then again, this is Jake, minimal words, more action. I guess the fact that he's still walking beside me, still talking to me means that he's okay with my explanation.

I don't really know, but now my mind's full of other thoughts.

Of Project S and what it could mean to the Mystyx.

It takes another hour and three phone calls to Lindsey before she finally meets us at the end of the street where Mrs. Hampton lives. It's not really a street, more like a long winding road that ends with this big dark house with windows that look like eerie golden eyes. It makes me shiver every time I see it.

Lindsey's ponytail bounces as she walks fast to get to us. She's wearing cutoff shorts and a black-and-purple striped tank top with black sneakers and no socks. She looks like she could be an elementary school student with her short stature and cutie-pie face.

"Okay, what's the big emergency?"

"What took you so long?" Jake asks as soon as she slows in front of us.

She rolls her eyes but answers him anyway. "I couldn't just walk out. I'm not…I don't have…" She sighs, then pushes her bangs back from her forehead. "Look, it's just not that simple for me. But I'm here now. So what's up?"

The sky seems darker, darker than it should be for still so early in the evening. And I can't see my moon at all. Not any parts of it. The full moon isn't for a few days but I don't even see the quarter moon. Nothing but blackness. I feel a little unsteady in its absence.

"Ah, maybe we should take this little meeting some place else," I suggest, looking around and catching a tiny breeze against my neck. There's a message on that breeze, a chilly warning that makes me tremble. All the while my *M* is still warming the skin at my side.

Jake reaches up, rubs his arm through his hoodie, and I know he's feeling the warmth, too. I've never seen Lindsey react to her *M,* so I look down at her ankles. She's moving, shuffling from one foot to the other like she's nervous or something.

"You okay?" I ask.

She nods her head, her ponytail bobbing along also. "Fine."

"Let's go in here," Jake suggests.

"Here" is the old canning warehouse. They used to can sardines in there years and years ago. I guess they positioned the warehouse here so the stench wouldn't filter throughout the entire town on a daily basis. We're almost in no-man's-land out here by Lindsey's house. In fact, I'm guessing that if we walked through Mrs. Hampton's house straight out the back door, we could step off the land and swim right in the Atlantic Ocean. Creepy.

Anyway, the company left long before I was born. But the smell stayed. My nose crinkles as we step inside the dark, damp space. There's not much light in here as the only lamppost on the street is a distance away. But that's okay. We don't need light to talk.

Jake does the honors, giving Lindsey an abbreviated version of what we suspect. She listens closely before saying a word.

"You've gone up against this Darkness before. How do we fight it this time?"

I shrug. "We really didn't know how to fight it the last time. It just sort of happened."

Lindsey blows air out of her mouth, so hard it ruffles the hair on her forehead. "We've gotta be more prepared than that this time. My bet is it grows stronger every day, with every attack. And it wants something, it seems like it wants something from us."

"Then why keep taking over other bodies?" Jake asks, pacing back and forth in what looks like an imaginary box. "Why not just come right at us?"

"It is," I say. "It's following me around town like a stalker. Every time I look up I see it. It knows who and what we are."

"That's why I said it wants something from us," Lindsey adds. "But how does Mr. Bryant fit in?"

"He knows about us, too," I say. "He knows that power is coming from those strange storms. Maybe he wants to harvest the power for himself."

"Maybe he's already harvested it and it's inside of Franklin," Jake offers.

"No." Lindsey shakes her head. "I don't think so. Not yet. If he did, wouldn't he be broadcasting it? Trying to sell it or at least get credit for the discovery? No, I think he's close to finding out about the power, but needs the Carrington money to get him there."

Jake smirks. "And her dad will probably give it to him, then we'll all be in deep trouble. Because you know what'll happen once news of this gets out."

As much as I want to counter what Jake's saying, I can't. The fact of the matter is it's probably true. "Once news gets out, we'll be outcasts," I say quietly.

"Some of us are used to that already," Jake tosses my way.

I open my mouth to speak, but Lindsey lifts a hand and steps between me and Jake. "Enough. We're all outcasts. Think about it. Who's gonna want to be around us when they find out we've got supernatural powers—except the wrong kind of people? It's time we started thinking along those lines and stop letting all this other stuff interfere with what we need to do."

Jake and I both look over at her, and I'm wondering again

where she came from and what her real purpose here is. Then I shrug, maybe she's right. She belongs to our little group of outcasts just as much as the rest of us.

Then we hear the creaking of sorely unoiled hinges, and all three of us go still. Nobody knows we're here, so who's at the door?

In the next seconds, Krystal comes running inside, stopping only because Jake reaches out his arms and catches her against his chest. She's breathing fast, almost like she ran all the way here from her house—which would be a really long run, and Krystal is not on the track team.

"They…know." She tries to talk and catch her breath at the same time. "They…know…about…us," she finally manages.

"Hold on, take a deep breath," Jake tells her. She stands up straight but stays in Jake's grasp as he rubs a hand down her back. "That's it, take it slow."

She swallows, blinks once or twice, then tries again. "They know about us. I saw them sitting in a room looking at a screen. Then he puts in a flash drive and on the screen appears a presentation called 'Project S.' It goes through several storms and well-known events in time. It explains how those events equate to something real, something potentially dangerous to the entire world. Only we're not dangerous. Not us. The project isn't just about us."

"You had a vision," I say, taking a step closer to her.

She looks at me like I'm the last person she wants to be talking to but then just rolls her eyes and admits, "Yeah."

"Who was in it?" Lindsey asks.

"Your father," she spits my way, but I stand perfectly still. I keep looking right at her. I am not responsible for my father's actions, and I won't keep apologizing for things I don't have any control over.

So I say, "And who else?"

She gets quiet then, and I know what she's going to say even before she says it.

"Walter Bryant."

She nods her head positively.

"Jeez." Jake lets out a whoosh of air and goes back to his little stalking box.

"There were others but I don't know who they are," she says. "And there's something else."

Jake's still pacing. Me and Lindsey ask in unison, "What?"

"The creatures, the ones we talked about the other day, that only you and I can see. They were there, too."

A slivery chill rolls down my spine. At my side, my fingers clench and unclench. "You only see them in your visions, right?"

Krystal nods.

"And you see them where?" Lindsey asks me.

I shrug, but it's anything but nonchalant. "Anywhere. I mean, I haven't seen any since we were at the mall that night. But I don't think I have to be any specific place to see them. They're here, walking along the streets with us."

Jake's voice erupts with worry and frustration. "Then what the hell are they?"

"And what do they want?" Krystal asks.

Lindsey's rubbing her arms and now sinking slowly to the floor where she crosses her legs. Then one of her hands slides down her leg to cup her ankle. The one with her *M*.

She cringes as if in pain. I know exactly what she's feeling because I'm feeling it, too. At my side.

Lindsey's *M* is glowing. A deep intense purple color that provides additional light in the dark warehouse.

If I lift up my shirt, I'm sure mine is glowing pink.

Turning to Jake, I know his is glowing green even though he keeps moving so I can't really see. Krystal isn't even bothering to hide it. She takes a step closer to me and Lindsey then holds out her hands.

Lindsey stands and reaches out, taking one. They both stare at me expectantly. I'm not sure where Krystal and I stand on a personal level. What I am absolutely positive about is at this moment we're committing to each other, to our power and to whatever lies ahead of us.

I take Krystal's other hand, and the heat at my side simmers to a comfortable warmth that immediately spreads throughout my body.

*Be vigilant.*

I hear the voice I've heard so many times before. But this time, Krystal and Lindsey hear it, too. I can tell by the way their gazes shoot up, back and forth from me to the other.

"Did you—" Lindsey begins, but I'm already nodding my head.

Krystal nods, too. "So did I."

The three of us look at Jake, who has stopped pacing but now has his hands thrust into his front pants pockets. "Yeah, I hear it," he says and moves closer to us.

Breaking through the clasp of Krystal and Lindsey's hands, Jake makes our circle complete.

And there we stand, in the dark warehouse, our symbols glowing, words of encouragement from the unknown source still echoing throughout the drafty old space. We are the Mystyx and we are in this together. No matter what.

# twenty-one

2nite @ 8 main street

That's the text I get as soon as I sit down in first period. I'm a bundle of nerves today and with good reason. At eight o'clock tonight, we're planning to break into Walter Bryant's office and steal his flash drive. Never mind that this flash drive might expose us and our powers to the world. I'm turning into a thief.

Never would have guessed it of myself, but then again, I never would have guessed I'd be a part of a group of supernaturals charged with saving the world. That sounds like a big job, and I guess in retrospect it really is. I know we're just in Lincoln, a small town on the east coast, but there's something here that wants to get rid of us. There's got to be a reason why.

It's raining really hard today. Looking to my left, I can see out the window that the faculty parking lot is being drenched with heavy raindrops. The sky is a sickly gray color, and to make matters worse, the wind just kicked up a notch so that the driving sheets of rain are now blowing around like a water hose on the loose. Several late students are running, books on top of their heads—as if that's really going to help—trying to make it into the building as quickly as they can.

I shiver. Not because I'm cold but because of the trickling

sense of dread each falling raindrop deposits inside me. It's just a rainstorm, and yet I feel something different. Something more. Tingling sensations move throughout my body as if I'm growing or something inside me is expanding.

The Power.

The door to the classroom slams, and in walks a tall woman with a briefcase in one hand and a mug in the other. She's not Mrs. Copaceptic, and the rest of the class reacts to the substitute with glee. Me, I just stare at her.

And when she puts her briefcase down on the desk, takes a sip out of her mug and puts that down as well, she does the most alarming thing. She stares right back at me.

Only she doesn't have eyes.

I know it shouldn't scare me, considering all the things I've been seeing lately, but it does. So I scream. And scream until I feel hands on my shoulders shaking me and voices around me calling my name.

Then I stop screaming. Well, at least my mouth closes. The sound is still reverberating in my head. Somebody is carrying me—quickly because I feel a slight breeze against my face.

I'm lying down now, in a dark room. My chest and my throat hurt from screaming so loud and so long. Other than that, I'm lying perfectly still. My eyes are blinking but not seeing a thing. Then they're closed, and I'm floating.

It's familiar to me now because I know where I'm going. Only I don't know who or what I'll see or hear this time when I get there.

"He is not alone."

I hear her and sigh with relief. I don't think I could have stood it if it was the Darkness again. Something like creepy overload would definitely have taken over me then.

"You told me that already," I say, getting tired of this drop-a-hint game she's playing.

No, I can't see her, just that blinding light again. But I don't look away. I stare forward because whenever she decides to show her face I want to see it.

"He won't stop unless you stop him."

"And just how do you expect us to do that? And why is it our job anyway?"

There is a pause.

"It is her curse and her blessing, I guess."

"Whose? Styx?"

"You are a quick one."

Inside, I feel good that I was right. We are connected to the goddess Styx and her river. "Why would she curse us? How could she curse us when she lived so long ago?"

"Her curse will last as long as the threat is living. He will not stop."

I nod my head, tired of her saying this. "Unless we stop him, I know all that. What I want to know is why? Why us? Why now?"

"Like the sun and the moon, it just is."

"What just is?"

"Styx's curse. Her power. Your duty."

"I want to know more about the curse, about how we got this power. What did Styx do to the weather to make us get this way?"

"Not now," the voice says, and I know she's getting ready to fade.

"Wait, I have more questions."

"Questions will not help you right now. Stop him first."

It goes all black again and I curse. This is one crappy deal we've been dealt. Stop him first, before anybody tells us exactly why we are. It just is, she said. Yeah, well, I don't like that answer. But to get more answers I guess we'd better do what she says since she's the only one who seems to know anything.

Now I'm starting to wonder who "she" is in all this.

"*Princesa, princesa,* wake up now."

I know that voice. Cracking one eye open, I try to smile at Casietta's obviously concerned face as she looks down at me.

"That's a good girl," she croons and wipes a palm against my cheek. "You wake up so we can go home."

There are a lot of students who would kill for someone to come and take them out of school early. But not me. If Casietta takes me home now, she won't let me out of her sight for the rest of the night. And I won't be able to break into Mr. Bryant's office.

I struggle to sit up with Casietta next to me on the side of the small cot. "No. I don't need to go home. I'm fine."

"You just screamed down the entire classroom. I'm surprised the windows didn't break." That is Nurse Hilden speaking with her pinched face and broken-off fingernails. "I think you should go home."

"No," I say, adamantly shaking my head. "I'm okay, just had a bad scare, that's all. It's fine now."

"What scared you?" Casietta asks.

I hesitate. This isn't something I can tell Casietta. I know this and yet I still want to. "Something just didn't look right and it freaked me out," I say instead.

Casietta's dark eyes narrow as she continues to stare at me. "Did not look right? Some*thing* or some*one?*"

All right, I've been thinking something freaky was going on with Casietta since her warning the other day. Now I'm sure she knows more than she's letting on. Why else would she ask me that question? So I decide to test the waters.

"Some*one.*"

Casietta's lips close in a tight line. Her hair is pulled back so tight her face looks pinched. She's wearing a floral dress with the same black leather purse she's carried ever since I can remember on her left arm. "What did they look like?"

Narrowing my eyes at her, I'm trying to figure out what to say or what not to say. I don't want her to take me home, and I definitely don't want her to call my father and tell him he needs to take me to a nuthouse. But something tells me none of that's going to happen now.

"Like she didn't belong here." I lower my voice because I don't want Ms. Hilden to hear me.

Casietta nods, her lips still tight, her eyes closing slowly, then opening the same way.

"What do you know, Casietta? What is it you're not telling me?"

"Not here," she whispers back, then takes a deep breath and releases it. She lifts her hand, touching her palm to my head. Then, speaking in a regular tone, she says, "You don't have a fever. I guess if you feel you are okay, it is safe for you to stay in school."

The way she says "safe" tells me she knows a lot. "Later, when I get home, we'll talk?"

Casietta nods. "I will see you at home after school.

"Mr. Lycanian will pick you up," she says, then gives me a hug.

It's a super tight hug, like the ones people give you when somebody dies.

I just nod my head as she lets me go.

"Then it's back to class for you," Ms. Hilden says, and Casietta walks quietly out of the office.

I stare at the doorway long after she's gone, wondering what I'm going to find out when I go home and talk to her.

Wondering how, yet positively sure, Casietta knows about my powers and what's going on around Lincoln.

The rest of the school day seems to drag along, sort of like the last day before winter break. Somehow the six-hour day feels like it's lasting more like twelve hours instead. But the final bell rang with definitiveness about five minutes ago. I make record time dropping books off to my locker, keeping what I'll need to study over the weekend, and head out toward the parking lot.

That's when I hear it.

The sound is muffled but it's definitely a scream. Every nerve in my body is instantly on alert. I turn in the direction that I hear the sound and am about to walk that way when someone grabs my arm.

"It's Krystal," Jake says, his fingers tightening on my arm.

Lindsey comes up on the other side of me. "Did you see her?"

"No. I just heard a scream. How do you know it's Krystal?" I ask Jake.

His lips are drawn as his eyes rake the parking lot and pause toward the line of trees at the end of the school grounds.

"There!" he yells, then takes off running.

Lindsey and I only pause a second before we're running across the parking lot right behind him. We get to the gate that separates the school property from the woods. I can teleport to the other side. Jake already jumped over the gate as if it were nothing more than a bag in the street. Lindsey climbs over, surprisingly very agile and picks up right behind me.

The trees are sort of thin at first. Then, the deeper into the woods we get, the thicker they are. We're both just following Jake's lead. I can't see Krystal or anything else besides him. He said he could feel that it was Krystal. I trust his feelings. And a few seconds later I come to a stop just before crashing into Jake's back as he stops ahead of me. Lindsey comes up beside me again just a little more out of breath than I am.

Krystal's back is against a huge tree, and Franklin's standing right in front of her, his hands on her shoulders.

"Let her go!" Jake says, and from behind I can feel the waves of tension coming off his body. I put a hand on his shoulder, hoping that will calm him down.

Franklin doesn't seem to hear him. He's wearing dark pants and a tight T-shirt. His arms are absolutely ripped, muscles so thick and bulging that the material of the shirt strains over them. This is not the Franklin I'm used to seeing. Everything about him seems different.

"I need you," he's saying to Krystal.

"No! Stop!" Krystal argues back, trying to release herself from his grasp. Her hair's fallen loose from the ponytail she was wearing today, her eyes more than a little frantic as she looks at this person we thought was just a normal boy.

Even though Franklin's holding Krystal up against that tree with her feet not even touching the ground, it looks like it's taking little effort. Keeping one hand on her shoulder to make sure she's pushed firmly against the tree, he reaches up to her face, his fingers dragging along her skin.

"I...need...you," Franklin says again, and I realize that not only is his appearance different, but so is his voice.

"Something's wrong with him," Lindsey whispers from behind me. "I can't really see his mind, but it's a lot of rage, a lot of dark anger around him."

The air around us is utterly still, and the sky is that drab gray color. It feels like we're in a box, trapped with our power on one side and something bigger and darker on the other.

"No!" Krystal screams, and Jake makes a move forward.

I grab him by both arms because that's what it takes to keep him from running over there. "You don't know what's in him, Jake. You don't know what he can do to you."

"I'm not worried about what he'll do to me, I'm worried about Krystal. He's hurting her!" And there's this sound that comes from Jake's chest that isn't good at all.

Krystal yells again, and we all look over to see Franklin's fingers move closer to her eye.

"I…need…you…now," he roars and sticks his fingers into Krystal's eye.

"Oh my god! He's gonna take them out. He needs them, was told to get them. I can see it. Krystal sees it and I can see her mind." Lindsey pushes past us and moves toward Krystal and Franklin.

In the next instant, she's blown off her feet, sliding along the ground like a batter going into third base. Jake pulls away from my grasp, and I fall forward on my knees trying to stop him. But there's no stopping Jake. Not this time. In two long strides, he's right behind Franklin, grabbing him up by the back of his collar and pulling him off Krystal.

She falls to the ground, gasping for air and instantly reaching up to her eyes—I guess to make sure they're still there. Lindsey scrambles over to her.

Pulling myself up, I head right for Jake who is still holding Franklin in his grip. That is until Franklin twists in Jake's grasp, opens his mouth and spits out thick black smoke that gets in Jake's eyes and has him stumbling backward. Falling to the ground, Franklin lands right on his feet like he was only levitating the whole time. I get a little closer, only to be knocked back down on my butt like I'd run into some sort of invisible shield.

Franklin throws back his head and laughs. And I know that sound. It's not Franklin's.

His eyes are changing right in front of me. The color is shifting from brown to yellow, to gold, to something iridescent, then to absolutely nothing. No eyes. Just like the bodies they found from that religious retreat.

"You can't win," Franklin's mouth opens, and he talks in the voice of the Darkness that's been following me.

The ground is now dark beneath my feet. Black smoke swirls all around us, rising up our legs like shackles. Krystal and Lindsey are still huddled by the tree. Jake is up now, fists clenching at his sides. He wants to charge Franklin—I can tell by the expression on his face—but something's stopping him. Probably the same shield that's keeping me down.

"No. You won't win!" I shout back because with the black smoke comes this weird howling sound, like a bunch of wounded animals crying out into the air.

"It is mine. It's always been mine. You can't take it away. I don't care what powers she's given you. She couldn't beat me and neither can you!" The voice roars through Franklin, his body shaking with the urgency of the words.

The wind starts to blow, black smoke whirling all around. I wish we had active powers, at least one of us. I mean, Jake can fight with his super strength, but he can't move. I can teleport, but not now, not through this shield. How are we supposed to beat this thing if we have no defenses against it?

I don't know the answers. I just know we're supposed to do something. So I concentrate. I think about getting past this shield, breaking it down or possibly just getting closer to Franklin's body. There has to be a way to get this Darkness out of him. Maybe if we'd done that when Mr. Lyle was possessed, this would all be over. But now is no time for regrets.

Closing my eyes, I call on everything that's inside me. I pull from everything I know: we are the Mystyx, our power stems from the goddess Styx and her river that was toxic, we are chosen to fight this Darkness, to win the battle between good and evil. We have to do something.

And as I crack my eyes open again, my body trembling with power, I feel the heat at my side. Spears of light come from each of us, from our birthmarks, cutting through the dark smoke. On impulse I take a step, and then another, and when I'm not knocked down again, I break into a run. Jake follows my lead, and we both crash into Franklin's body at the same time. Only by then, the body is reduced to nothing.

Dark smoke lifts into the air, trickling through our grasp and headed upward to the sky. The laughter sounds and echoes throughout the wooded area.

"You won't win!" it says, and all the smoke is swooped up into a thick cloud that floats away.

We're all too stunned to move. So we just sit or stand in that clearing in the woods. Gradually the air clears, the sky, which was a dismal gray, opens to a wan blue. The smoke is gone, but we all act as if it's still there, as if this thing that's taunting us is still right here. We're so quiet, not really sure what to say.

Jake wants to move closer to Krystal, to touch her, to make sure she's all right. But he remains still where he stands, slipping his hands into his pockets. My heart instantly goes out to him as I think I know what he's feeling. Wanting somebody but not being able to just say it, to just be with them. I'm thinking of Antoine again and the argument we had. He's right about me playing games and being ashamed of being with him. I shouldn't be. He's a cool guy and his aunt's really nice. I shouldn't care what my parents or anyone else will say.

"He won't stop." Lindsey breaks the silence. Leaves and twigs crunch beneath her feet as she stands, reaching a hand out to help up Krystal, who was still sitting on the ground beside her. "He'll come back because our power is what keeps him from gaining his strength. As long as we're alive, he can't get what he wants."

"And what's that?" Krystal asks, brushing the dirt and crap off her clothes. "I mean, what is it that he wants that we can stop him from getting?"

"More power," Jake says quietly. "There are three things worth fighting for—money, power and respect. I doubt he needs the money or the respect. It's the power that's driving him. But somebody's keeping it from him."

Krystal nods, her hands and attention having gone from her mussed clothes to Jake. "Somebody created a final barrier so that he wouldn't be able to get that power. Ever. We're that barrier. We were created to stop him. But by who?"

"Styx," I say. "She did something, cursed the weather or something so that we would be created to fight him when he came for the power."

We all take a minute to let that sink in. I think we know it's right. Some of the holes we've had in our theory are finally filling up.

"Created by a goddess," Lindsey says on a whoosh of breath. "Cool."

I laugh, and then so do Jake and Krystal. I know it's probably not the most opportune time to do such a thing, but it just sort of bubbles out, and before I know it or can stop it, everybody is laughing. In the midst of all this unknowing and turmoil, only Lindsey could think it was cool.

And while I know it's far from over, it feels good to have this one moment, alone with the Mystyx, laughing, for once.

# twenty-two

Later that evening when I arrive at the office building on Main Street, I see that Lindsey is already there.

"Mr. Bryant's already left for the evening. He seemed kind of nervous, something about meeting bigwigs in Washington," she tells me as we creep around to the side of the building.

It's really dark out tonight. Even though it's only like ten minutes to eight, the sky is already fully dark as if it were midnight. Before I left the house I heard on the six o'clock news that there was a thunderstorm watch. But it doesn't seem like thunderstorm weather to me.

"Who is he meeting with?" I ask.

Lindsey shakes her head. "I couldn't get that much."

When I look back at her she's frowning. "You okay?"

"Uh-huh," she says, but I don't really believe her.

She looks a little distant, like she's thinking about something, trying to figure it out. I don't know what it is, so I figure we'll deal with the matter at hand, then deal with her personal problems.

"Have you heard from Krystal and Jake?" I hadn't talked to either of them since we'd left the woods and gone our separate ways. I'd offered everyone a ride home, but they declined. I think we kind of wanted a moment alone to think about what had just happened. So I didn't push.

"We're here," Jake says from behind me.

I turn and see him and Krystal walking towards us.

"So what's the game plan?" Krystal asks, but she's not looking at me, so I figure we must still be on the outs.

"Mr. Bryant's already gone, so it's clear for us to go in. Did you bring the flash drive?" she asks Jake.

"Yeah, I got it." He pulls it out of his pocket and shows us the small black device that looks just like the one in Mr. Bryant's office.

"What about the security guards? How do we get past them?" Krystal says.

"Shoot, didn't think about them." Jake frowns.

"Sasha, you go," Lindsey suggests. "Use your power to get into the office. Nobody will even know you're in the building."

"Ah, okay," I say, not sure I'm liking the plan where I do this alone. Still, I hold out my hand for the flash drive.

He gives it to me and says, "Be careful."

"No problem," I say, like sure, I teleport into offices and play the switcheroo game every day.

I take a few steps back from them and close my eyes. In seconds, I'm in Mr. Bryant's office by myself.

Because it's so dark outside, it's even darker in here. The last thing I want to do is turn on a light and risk somebody just happening to drive by and see it on, so I'm working on memory alone as I walk around.

"Ow!" I hit my knee on the desk that I knew was there but misjudged the distance.

Okay, so the file cabinet was across the room from the desk. I turn around, keeping my hands behind me so I can feel the desk. I'm thinking about seven steps were what I took before I was standing right next to Jake, who was near the file cabinet.

Counting off, I stop right at seven and reach my hands out in front of me. I don't feel anything.

"Crap." I sigh and think of what I'm going to do next. Nothing bright is coming to mind. I just keep returning to the idea of turning on that lamp.

But then my side starts to warm and I start to smile. This power really is starting to work in conjunction with my emotions. My shirt is tucked into my jeans, so I hurriedly pull it out, bringing it around the front of me and tying a quick knot with the excess material. I'm glowing now, or at least my *M* is, and the fluorescent pink light is giving me just enough illumination to see.

The cabinet is just to my left about another step or two. I'm happy to learn my memory wasn't that far off. I don't want to waste any more time, so I move to the cabinet and pull open the top drawer. My fingers quickly whisper over the files, stopping on the one marked "Project S." I'm still trying to figure out why *S?* Maybe I'm just so hung up on our *M. S* could stand for supernatural, I guess.

That's what I'm thinking as I pull the file free from the cabinet and open it up. The flash drive had been in a small pouch in the front inside flap of the file folder. "Had been" being the operative phrase.

It's not there.

My fingers move over the pouch, but it's empty.

Flipping through the pages to the back of the file folder, I see another pouch, but that's empty, too.

I want to curse or scream. Or both. Instead I simply sigh.

Where is it? Did Mr. Bryant know that we were in here before? Did he know that we were on to him?

Closing the file cabinet, I'm thinking of how I'm going to tell the others that this little operation was a bust when I appear again in front of them.

"Did you get it?" Jake asks first.

The others look at me expectantly, and I feel like such a heel to be bearing the bad news. "No. It wasn't there."

"What do you mean it wasn't there? Where is it?"

I sigh. "If I knew that, Jake, I'd teleport there and get it."

"Bryant took it," Krystal says. "You think he knew someone was in his office? What if there're cameras in there?"

We're quiet because, the fact is, Jake and I never gave that possibility any thought.

Then I shake my head. "If Mr. Bryant knew I was in his office, I'm sure he would have told my dad."

Jake smirks. "And your dad would have done what?"

"Let's just say I'm sure I wouldn't be out here with you tonight if he knew."

And speaking of my dad…

"We should go back to my place."

"For what?" Jake and Krystal ask in unison.

"Because I think that's where we can get some more answers." Dinner had been already prepared by the time I'd made it home from school. But Casietta hadn't been there. Her and I were supposed to talk when I came home, but she'd conveniently disappeared. I hadn't been too pressed about it at the time because I'd wanted to be alone in my room until it was time for me to slip out and come downtown. But now I'm beginning to wonder what she's hiding.

"I don't want to go to your house," Krystal says adamantly.

"I don't think we have a choice," Lindsey says. "Look, we're all in this together. If there are answers back at Sasha's house, then that's where we should go."

Krystal rolls her eyes. Jake shrugs. And I finally lead the way.

★ ★ ★

Nobody greeted us when we walked through the front door. And we'd been in the family room for more than fifteen minutes before Casietta came in.

"Your parents are out for the night," she said, glancing around the room.

The furniture in here is all Italian leather, soft to the touch, comfortable to sit on but the weirdest shade of green I've ever seen. It never fails to amaze me, when I come in here, how these colors don't quite seem to mix. The thick rug covering glossy hardwood floors is dark orange, almost brown, I guess. The curtains are a combo of the two, and the paintings throughout add even more colors. It is like this is the one room my mother forgot to have professionally decorated.

Jake and Krystal sit next to each other on the love seat, while Lindsey moves about in her usual graceful manner. Occasionally her hand reaches, touches, the back of a chair, a pillow, the base of the coffee-colored lamp on the end table near the window. She has something on her mind, something other than what happened tonight. I'm almost positive of that fact.

Casietta stands in the middle of the room now. Her face looks worried, and she's rubbing her hands together in front of her.

I am about to say something when Mouse comes in. My mouth closes instantly because Mouse never comes into the house. Ever.

But he is here now, closing the door quietly behind him.

"He's taken another one," he says solemnly, looking at Casietta.

So I look at Casietta, hoping for a clue to what he's talking about.

"That bus was coming back from a religious retreat. They

were just children learning how to do good. It's not right," she says, turning away, then walking toward the window where Lindsey is now standing.

The minute Casietta's close, Lindsey reaches out a hand and touches her arm.

"Your grief is overwhelming. But your fear is greater. What is it that's scaring you so?"

With an astonished look, Casietta glares at Lindsey, then her whole body seems to deflate as she sighs. "You have the power to see my thoughts. I wondered what you'd bring to them when you came."

"You knew Lindsey was a Mystyx?" I ask.

"I know who and what all of you are. The question is how did you know?"

Jake shrugs. "We found my great-grandmother's journal and then my grandfather told us some stuff."

Casietta chuckles. "I knew Louis would never be able to keep his mouth closed. Talks too much he does. Always has."

"You know Jake's grandfather?" Krystal asks incredulously.

"Yes," Casietta says, nodding her head. There's a swishing sound as she starts to walk from the window back to the center of the room. I think it's the nylons that she always wears beneath whatever floral dress she chooses for the day. "We share a common goal."

"And what's that?" I ask.

"To protect you. All of you."

This is Mouse speaking in that eerily deep voice of his that doesn't really sound like English but isn't any foreign accent that I've been able to figure out.

"How are you going to protect us?" Jake asks.

Lindsey chimes in, "And what are you protecting us from?"

Casietta takes a deep breath, then releases it. "She was supposed to explain it all to you. But things are moving a lot faster than any of us thought they would."

"He is ready," Mouse says.

I'm still amazed that he's in here. And he looks so uncomfortable. Actually, he looks like he's taking up more space than is available in this room. Which is crazy since this is no small room. Still, Mouse looks oddly out of place.

"She knew this would happen. She knew he'd come for them. They're all that's stopping him."

Krystal clears her throat and raises her hand like she's in a classroom, and they—Casietta and Mouse—are the teachers. "Um, excuse me, but can somebody tell us what you're talking about?"

"You know what we are," I start saying, even though it's more than obvious that they know. I'm just trying to make sense of all this. How have Casietta and Mouse known all along? And do my parents know? "You've known all along and you never said anything to me."

Casietta begins shaking her head, the tight bun at the bottom not moving an inch. The droopy skin of her cheeks moves a bit, but her eyes remain steady as she stares at me. "They come to me in the middle of the night and wake me. They say, 'take her, you must take care of her.' I don't know what to do, but then she came to me, with so much bright light. She told me what would eventually happen and I believed her. I say I will take care of you."

"Who is 'she'? My mother?"

"Oh, no." Casietta starts shaking her head adamantly. "No, Señora, she did not know. Señor say it's not true. He think it is all not real."

"Wait a minute, I don't understand. If my mother didn't tell you to take care of me, who did?"

Casietta's gaze goes to Mouse who looks grim as he folds his arms over his chest.

"You have to go to her and ask for the truth. It is time. She will tell you."

"Okay, is anybody else in here tired of trying to figure out who 'she' is?" Jake says.

"I mean, really, why can't you just tell us?" Krystal counters.

Lindsey just shakes her head. "They are bound by some kind of oath to keep quiet. It's like a shield up in their minds, blocking it out, so that just in case they were ever tempted to tell all, they can't."

With a sneaking suspicion of what's about to happen, I add, "Or they're just blocking you out."

Walking from where I was standing behind the couch, I stop right in front of Mouse. Saying I have to almost break my neck looking up at him is not an exaggeration. But I do it anyway because I want him to know how serious I am about this. "Who is 'she'? Is it Styx?"

"She asked you to come to her." I hear Casietta's voice from behind. "The message on the computer says for you to come to her for your answers. You read the curse on the letter so she knew it was time you all know the truth."

I'm going to have serious neck injuries after this night. I whip around fast to see Casietta. "You're talking about Fatima? She's the witch I contacted that lives in Bridgeport."

"No witch." Casietta nods. "Just a messenger."

"Contact her again, Sasha," Krystal says, coming to the edge of the chair, looking at me with a silent plea in her eyes. "Send her another email or something. Just get us some answers."

Okay, no pressure, right? Running my fingers through

my hair, I try to figure out what Casietta and Mouse are telling me and what I was already thinking was true. If Fatima
isn't a witch, then who is she? Maybe our powers aren't connected to witchcraft. Maybe everything we thought is wrong.
Maybe...

"Sasha," Casietta says. "You can contact her. You have done
it before without the computer."

Casietta, the woman who raised me in this house. The
one who taught me both Spanish and English, who cleaned
me up after I fell off my bike and busted both knees, the one
who talked to me about boys and girls and reproduction, the
one...who was right there after that first time. She's known all
along. She watched me grow, knowing that one day it would
come to this.

"You mean astral project? That's how I can contact her?"

Casietta nods her head in agreement.

Then I'm beginning to understand. "I've talked to her there
before."

"Yes," Casietta says. "You can do it again."

Mouse takes a step forward. "But this time we will watch
you. He is ready and he will act the moment he knows you
are there."

"We will all watch you this time to make sure you come
back. *Si?*"

Casietta's nodding around the room, waiting for everyone
to agree with her. Krystal is already standing up, shaking her
head positively.

"Yeah, we'll be right here," Lindsey says.

Jake stands last, looking a little uncertain but joining in
with everyone else.

I move to the couch, wondering if this is a good idea. Lying
down, I put my fear into words. "What can he do to me if he
catches me there?"

The room goes quiet. Jake, Krystal and Lindsey look to Casietta and Mouse for the answer.

Casietta closes her eyes. Mouse speaks up. "It is different there, rules are different."

That's way too cryptic for my liking. "And?"

"And he could kill you or capture you."

I swallow deep because I figured this was the answer. "Okay, and what does he gain if he does either of those things?"

"You," he says as he looks around at all of us, "are the only thing stopping him from what he wants. If he gets rid of you one by one or all together, he wins."

"But, I don't understand." My words are cut off when Mouse touches a hand to my forehead.

This is different. Mouse has never touched me before. Ever. His hand on me now feels really weird, heavy and cold like ice. I'm looking into his eyes and see how dark they are, how perfectly round and dark. His brows are thick and bushy, but that's all the hair he has on his head or his face. He's not frowning, just wearing a bland expression that I feel like I should understand.

"Close your eyes and concentrate," he says slowly.

It's like I'm being hypnotized by his eyes and the sound of his voice because I instantly close my eyes. I know where it is I want to go, but this is different from teleporting.

I don't focus on getting to the point. Instead, I focus on the power inside me, feeling it grow and spread throughout my body. I think this is like getting a blood transfusion. It's moving through my veins at record speed, touching every nuance of my soul. My limbs feel heavy, like they're sinking into the cushions of the chair.

I think I hear somebody soothing me, coaxing me to take my time. But the voices are growing distant. I'm traveling now, feeling the weightlessness of flying. A cool breeze swipes my face, ruffles my hair. I'm soaring, high above everything I know to be true. I'm leaving it behind, heading into the unknown—yet, familiar.

She's calling me. I guess it's Fatima or whoever she really is. I don't hear a voice, just feel this physical tug inside that wants me to keep going. I don't fight it, don't try to rationalize it. I just keep going.

# twenty-three

IT'S different this time, here on this astral plane. Before, it was either really dark or super bright.

Now it just looks normal. Well, as normal as possible for another plane. Everything is white, but it looks like I'm in a room. There are four walls, and although I can't see the outline of a door, there's a gold knob that sort of gives me the indication that I can get out if I want to.

I take a tentative step. The white floor seems solid even though it looks cloudy. Another breeze blows by, so force-ful that it makes me stumble. When I right myself, I see the smallest spot of light. I stop all movement, afraid that if I move I'll lose sight of it. But I don't because the small fleck of light grows and grows until its brightness is eventually tapped out, and in its place stands a woman.

As weird as all this seems, the woman looks rather normal. Her skin is the color of heavily creamed coffee, flawless and radiant. Her eyes are like this funny brown/gold combina-tion with thick perfectly arched brows that make me just a tad jealous. One of my eyebrows is always arched a bit higher than the other, whether I do them myself or go to the mall to have them done. Never could figure that out.

This woman, who I'm guessing is Fatima, is also tall, with a tiny waist and curvy hips. She's wearing a long multicolored skirt that's lifting in the constant, but substantially softened, breeze. Her top clings like a bodysuit and is as white as the walls. At her waist is a huge red belt, on both her wrists about three inches of silver bangles, and at her ears are chandelier earrings twinkling with a rainbow of colors. So, like I said, she looks perfectly normal, a bit colorful and eclectic, but still normal for the most part.

What I really mean is nobody would ever know she's a witch or whatever other unnatural thing she may be.

Unless they were here in this place, with the breeze moving around us both. This place that I've been to and seen a few times now and still have no idea where it is or why I can be here.

"It is called the Majestic," Fatima says, speaking in her real voice—not the sing-songy echo I've heard before—for the first time. "It is another plane between earth and the heavens."

And I'm here because? I don't actually say that because clearly I'm still reeling from actually being in her presence.

Fatima's small, pert lips spread into a smile. "You're here because you are one of them."

Gulping and taking a deep breath, I realize at some point I'm actually gonna need to start talking to her if I want the answers to my questions. Even though it kind of feels like she can read my mind like Lindsey. "One of who?"

"She said she would send protectors. She warned them not to cross her. And here you are." Both her arms stretch out towards me, her bangles clinking loudly.

"She who? And what are we supposed to be protecting? Look, forgive me, but I'm really confused here."

Fatima simply nods. "She said you would be. And that is why I am here. To help you and the others find your way. The challenge is big and dangerous. Without the proper knowledge, you will have a hard time succeeding."

"Then could you please give me the proper knowledge?" I

know that sounds sarcastic and is probably really disrespectful, but I'm tired of the games. I want answers.

"You all are very intuitive. You have already figured out who you are and what your symbol means and that you were sent here by Styx. Because of her curse, you and your friends are in a battle to save this earth."

"To save it from who?"

"He is very angry that his plan did not work, that Styx ultimately caught him. He will not stop until all power—light and dark—is his."

"Do you have power? Are you a witch?" This probably doesn't relate to the Mystyx and our overall goal, but I've got to know.

"I am what is called a Messenger. I am eternally pledged to do the will of the goddess."

"But you knew about Mary Burroughs and the letter. Was Mary a witch?"

"That is a mortal name given to one who holds power. There are many species of powerful beings, especially here in the Majestic. It is the home of the magical."

"Why am I the only Mystyx who can come here?"

"You are the only one of your friends who has astral projection power. Styx gave you all different powers so that, combined, you could complete the task."

"Those things that I saw, the faces of those people in the mall. What was that?"

She nods her head, and I expect those big dangly earrings to make a sound, but they don't.

"Because you can visit the Majestic, you can also see what others cannot. You can see the true being through the glamour they use on earth."

"So these are really magical beings and not real humans? And they're just walking alongside humans every day?"

She smiles. "See, very intuitive."

No, very out of my league, I'm thinking. Then I hurry up and push the thought from my mind. If she can see into my thoughts, I'd better not think too much right now.

"Krystal sees them, too."

"No. She has the power to see the undead and to see what may happen in the future. If she sees magical beings, it is because they are about to reveal themselves to you all in some way. Heed her warnings. They will be very accurate."

Now it's my turn to nod. Krystal can see future events. That's good to know, but very unsettling, considering the last couple visions she's had. "And Styx gave us these powers by using the weather?"

"It is difficult for the magical to mingle with the mortals. There is such a thick level of misunderstanding. Styx has power of the sun and the moon. The rest comes naturally."

"How?"

Fatima's head tilts, and for the first time I see the long strands of fiery red hair. It looks like when one of the Goth girls used packs of cherry Kool-Aid to dye her hair, except this looks soft and glittery, not stiff and matted. I wish I could touch it.

"You are a child of the moon, of what mortals call a subtle eclipse."

Her voice is kind of fading, the breeze blowing a bit stronger. "Wait! Why can't I stay as long as I like, ask all the questions I want?"

She chuckles, and this time it sounds like wind chimes. "I am not here to give you all the answers, only to keep you on the right track."

In essence, she is like the Good Witch Glinda in *The Wizard of Oz*—she could come in on a beam of light, say some lyrical words that have vague meaning and then disappear. I'm beginning to get the picture, whether I like it or not.

"Then just answer this, how do we stop him? How can the four of us alone defeat this Darkness or whatever he is."

"He is powerful and from the Underworld. He has the strength of many dark souls behind him. You must be careful and stand strong together. When the time comes, you will know what to do. Trust your hearts, your minds. They control your powers."

The breeze kicks up to full-fledged wind, pushing me back until I'm gliding along the clouded floor on my butt. Then the clouds from the floor begin to swirl, and suddenly I feel the lightness of floating once more. I'm on my way back, my mind is racing with Fatima's words, my heart thumping with the extra knowledge and yet ignorance of what is to come.

"Why were you sent to watch over me?" I ask Casietta that night.

Earlier, she'd made me, Krystal, Jake and Lindsey lunchmeat sandwiches and ordered us to eat them.

Then I'd said goodbye to the other Mystyx as Mouse had ushered them all to a car to take them home. After that, I showered and am now lying on my stomach across the bottom half of my bed, staring up at Casietta. She's picking up things, moving them around. Essentially she's keeping busy. She's been doing that since I came home tonight. I can tell there's more she hasn't told me.

Even now she doesn't answer my question but just hunches her shoulders.

"Does my father know that I'm a supernatural?"

"He knows danger might come for you. That is all."

"Is that really all he knows or is it all he wants to know?"

"He is a tough man, your papa. I do not understand him all the time."

"That's good because I don't ever understand him." I sigh, then roll over onto my back. "And my mother doesn't know."

"Your papa threaten to shoot anybody who tell her. So I keep my mouth shut."

"You're good at doing that, huh, Casietta?"

She stops then and turns to me. In her hand she's holding my robe and the jeans I just took off. She's rolling both the pieces in her arms now, her cheeks puffing with the exertion. "I do my job."

I nod. "And your job is to protect me. Well, who protects the other Mystyx?"

"They all have guardians."

"So you are mine. Who are the others?"

"I only know that fool Louis is supposed to watch out for Jake. He didn't watch his brother the way he was told, so I don't know why he have another chance with Jake. But it is not my place to complain."

I see. Mr. Kramer's brother William had the same super strength and telekinetic power that Jake does. But Mr. Kramer never had any power. I guess because he's a guardian. "And Krystal?"

"I don't know. She was not born here, so I do not know who was assigned to her. Lindsey either, she is a mystery."

I almost laugh at that one because I'm beginning to think the same thing about Lindsey. "What if Lindsey and Krystal hadn't come back to Lincoln, could Jake and I have fought this thing alone?"

"The goddess knows what she is doing."

Lying back on my pillow, I listen as Casietta fusses around my room a little longer. When she comes over to the bed, I close my eyes like I've fallen asleep. She pulls the covers up to my chin and tucks them tight at my sides, just like she used to do when I was younger. I don't mind because now I know why she's always gone the extra mile for me, why she's been more like a mother than my real one.

She's my guardian and Fatima is the Messenger. We're Mystyx, and we're to fight against some evil from the Underworld who pissed Styx off in some way a long time ago.

Wow, this has been some day.

*Darkness cannot drive out darkness; only light can do that. Hate cannot drive out hate; only love can do that.*

—Martin Luther King, Jr.

# twenty-four

ON Saturday morning I get up early, much earlier than normal, but that's because I have something to do. I quickly dress, then head straight downstairs to my father's office. Usually he's out by eight with the excuse that he's heading to the gym. But we have a gym in our house, right down those three steps on the side of the kitchen. It's huge and has everything the rinky-dink gym in town does, probably more. So a long time ago, I figured this was yet another excuse to get out of this house.

I'm probably the last person he's expecting to see, but he's been a priority on my list since learning of his plans for where to build this club.

"Daddy," I say when I step into his office.

He's behind his desk, already sifting through some papers, and he looks up at me with surprise.

This morning he looks a little older than usual, like maybe he has a lot on his mind. I imagine running a big company and managing all the money he does has to be stressful. And as I'm walking across the shiny wood floor to get closer to his desk, I realize I don't really know him all that well.

I mean, he's my father, I know that. He's been here all my life. But as for who Marvin Carrington really is, I have no clue. I don't know if there are certain foods he doesn't like, or what his favorites are. I've never seen him watching television or listening to music, so I don't know his preferences there either. He's like this stranger who shares a house with me and a last name. That's unsettling.

"I wanted to talk to you about the club."

He keeps his hair cut short, like a military cut. It used to be darker, but it's starting to show a lot of gray now. His eyes are dark, too, like a sea green, with no sparkle at all. His lips are thin and seem to thin out a little more as he sits back in his chair and continues to glare at me.

"Why are you up so early? Surely your mother has plans for you today. Something else you should be tending to."

I shake my head. "No. She has other plans today, but not me. So, like I said, I wanted to talk to you about the club."

"What about it?" He steeples his fingers together under his chin like he's some big-time mobster and I'm one of his minions coming to ask a favor.

"Jake Kramer is my friend. His family lives down by the tracks. He said that's where you want to build the club, that you're making them move. I don't think that's fair." This isn't how I'd planned to say this, but now that it's out, I'm glad.

"This is none of your concern," my father says, his voice a little gravelly.

"It is because Jake is my concern. He was my first friend here and I don't want to lose him."

"You will make other…more appropriate friends," he says seriously.

"Like Stephen Whitman the Fourth?" I snort.

"I'm afraid you may have already burned that bridge. But yes, friends of that nature." Then he leans closer, planting his elbows on his desk, his look even more disapproving of me than I've ever seen. "Don't think I don't know who you've been running around town with. The boy from the Tracks. The one from the gang. And those two new girls who just moved here that we know nothing about. I'd hoped your mother would have gotten you and your choice of friends under control by now."

So hurt am I by his vague and narrow-minded assessment of my friends, I lash out without even considering who I'm talking to. "She has no control over who my friends are. I associate with who I want. And you have no right to judge people you don't even know!"

"I have every right," he roars right back. "I live in this town. Most of my money has gone into building it up to what it is today. Do you think I like having all these others just crawl in here and take what is rightfully mine?"

He's crazy. In this instant, I know this to be true. If someone on the streets had told me this, I probably would have felt compelled to defend him—I mean, we do share the same blood and all that. But he is definitely not in his right mind to really believe what he's saying.

"It's just money, Dad. All you have is money. You don't have any real friends and you don't have a real family. We're just like statues that you like to move around when you can. It's actually really sad."

"You're really young and naive and this conversation is over. Leave my business to me."

I shake my head, knowing what I must do. It wasn't a part of my original plan to persuade him to leave Jake's property alone, but I feel like I have no other choice. I'm doing exactly what Fatima said, using my heart and my mind to do what needs to be done.

On legs stronger than they've ever been, I push the chair back slowly. His eyes rise, following my movements. "I may be young and probably a little naive where you're concerned but I'm dead serious about my request. Leave Jake's property alone. Find someplace else to build your club."

"Go to your room!" he yells.

But I have no intention of doing his bidding. Instead, I close my eyes and disappear, reappearing right beside him where I put a hand on his shoulder.

He jumps, his hand flailing out and knocking over the coffee cup that was on his desk. He's looking at me with just a hint of disbelief and a lot of fear. This is my father. My goal shouldn't be to scare him, it should be to look up to him, to love him. But he's not worthy of that. He's cold and manipulating, and it's time for that to stop.

"If Jake's house is torn down to build this club, I'll tell everyone your secret."

"Wh-what are you talking about?" he stutters.

I smile, then close my eyes and appear right next to the window where I pull the curtains open. "I'll tell everyone your daughter is a supernatural. That your flesh and blood is not normal."

He stands up quickly, too quickly because his chair gets caught on his legs. He kicks at it until it falls over.

"You're crazy! You're possessed! I told them that when you were born."

Tilting my head to the side, I can see clearly now that he'd probably said those very same words. Funny, they should hurt my feelings coming from the man who is supposed to be my father. But they don't. I can see his fear and his disbelief and know that if I weren't the one with the power, I would probably feel the same way. No, that's not true. I'm not like him. I can accept other people's differences and not judge them for it. Unfortunately, Marvin Carrington cannot. It's a shame we can't choose our parents.

"I am what I am and you've known it all my life. You chose to ignore it and me because you don't understand it. But it's not going away. And if you don't leave Jake's land alone, I'm going to share it with the world. Now, how many investors do you think you'll get then? How many clients will you lose, Daddy?"

I don't know what's got into me, but it feels good. I'm standing up for what I believe. Sure, I'm threatening my father in the process, with a secret I have no intention of revealing, but I'm betting he won't call my bluff. This image he's created for himself is far too important.

"You can't. It would kill your mother."

"It would destroy you, just as you're planning on destroying the lives of the people who live in those homes. Think about it, Dad. The choice is yours—their lives or yours?" And just for dramatics I disappear and reappear right in front of his desk, taking a seat in the chair I'd sat in before.

His shaky fingers are gripping his tie, acting as if it needs straightening when it doesn't. "You don't know what you're doing. You don't know what you're playing with. This isn't a joke, Sasha. It's not a game."

Don't I know it. If it were, I'd definitely be quitting by now. Running from possessed birds, fighting some dark entity that wants to kill me, are not normal pastimes for a teenage girl. But like I say to him in reply, "It is what it is, Dad. Do we have a deal?"

Reaching behind him, he finds his chair, then plops down into it. "Not a word of this to your mother. None of it, do you hear me?"

"What? You don't want even her to know who and what her daughter really is?" Now that *does* hurt. She's my mother, but this is why she treats me like I'm her hobby instead of her child—because he wants her to.

"She won't understand like I did. You were the one thing I asked of her and she gave me. Knowing your imperfections would kill her."

I'm biting my bottom lip to keep from crying. "My imperfections" is what he just said. I have imperfections. And he doesn't? Forget it, he's not worth my tears. "Build your club someplace else and leave my friends alone. I'll see who I want when I want without your interference. And no, I won't tell my mother of my imperfections." The words taste bitter in my mouth, but I say them, and leave them and this stranger alone.

The minute I close the door behind me, I want to scream. I want to run out and find my mother and scream at her for tolerating his controlling ways and for not understanding me. But I know that none of it will work. Sometimes you can't change who or what people are. If that were possible, Marvin Carrington certainly would have tried to change me.

# twenty-five

The next day they find the bus that the group who'd gone on the religious retreat used. It was deep in the woods just at the town border.

Nobody was inside.

Not the youth leader, Minister Hobbs, or the five remaining teenagers. The local police have instituted a full-on manhunt for someone they think might be responsible for the killing of the other two boys and possibly everyone from the bus. But they don't have a clue.

I don't either, but I know it's all connected to what we must do. He's sending us a message, although I'm not entirely sure what it is.

"Ever heard the saying 'your eyes are the windows to your soul'?" Mr. Kramer asks when we're sitting on the rickety old picnic table in Jake's backyard.

I came over to tell him that my dad wouldn't be bothering his family or their property any longer. Lindsey and Krystal were already here. I guess they'd been meeting without me, but I'm trying not to think too much of that. I understand things have been a little strained between us for a few days. A lot of that having to do with me being torn between working with Alyssa and my parents with the club and then the Antoine issues. Jake probably felt like I was betraying him in some way, and I guess so did Krystal. But I wasn't. I never would. I wonder if they know that now.

"Yeah, I've heard of it," Jake answers, getting up to help his grandfather down the steps. He's using his cane today, but he's moving a lot slower than normal.

"He needs the souls, needs to take them out so he can possess the body. That's how he gets them to do his bidding."

Standing up to make space for Mr. Kramer on the edge of the bench, Lindsey asks, "Who, Mr. Kramer?"

"Him, the dark one that you need to stop. It's children that he seeks, ones your age. He's looking for the marked ones like you."

"Ones that have an M," Krystal says quietly. She's sitting on the opposite side of the picnic table, and Jake has just come and sat beside her.

Lindsey and I are on the side with Mr. Kramer, who is now nodding his head with so much vigor I'm afraid he might make himself dizzy.

"When he doesn't find the mark, he takes their eyes which give him their soul."

"But why possess them?" I ask.

"Taking you out is not as easy as he planned. She cursed him good, she did." Mr. Kramer tilts his head back and laughs so hard the bottom row of his dentures shift, and he acts like he's coughing to cover his mouth.

"Why did she curse him? What did he do to her?"

"He got greedy, I suppose," Mr. Kramer said, and began looking around the yard. "Wanted more than he was supposed to have. More souls, I guess." Then Mr. Kramer is looking around like he sees something out here that we don't.

I follow his gaze, but I don't see anything. The wind does pick up, but it's been blowing all day. Real blustery-like, making any trash or debris on the ground circle in little pools.

Lindsey suddenly grabs her arms, like she's shivering. I see Krystal look from Lindsey to me and then around us. Jake's hands flatten on the table. He's looking down, but I can tell he's tensing.

"Styx has power over the moon and the sun. Her river also runs circles around the Underworld. Death, darkness and demons would have passed through her on a daily basis," says Mr. Kramer.

"You think this Darkness that's haunting us passed through her river at some point and pissed her off?" Jake asks, still not looking up at any of us.

"Everyone was afraid of her. The gods swore oaths by her. What if the oath sworn was broken?" Krystal asks.

Lindsey speaks, her hands still rubbing up and down her arms. "She would have cursed them to death probably." Her teeth start chattering, and she clamps her mouth shut.

"Unless the one who broke the curse is already dead. What if it's an immortal being we're fighting? How can we win?" Krystal asks just as a fierce gust of wind blows, knocking us all from the table.

I roll over on the ground and instantly look for Mr. Kramer to see if he's okay. He's lying flat on his back. I try to stand to get to him, but this wind is hellacious, knocking me right back down again. The sky has gone dark, heavy gray clouds are looming above, and the little circles of debris that were twirling on the ground earlier today are now lifting into tiny little cyclones all around the yard.

"What's happening?" Lindsey screams, her arms covering her head.

"I don't know," Krystal answers as she crawls under the table. Jake has made his way over to his grandfather and is pulling him toward the table where Krystal is. Joining the rest of the gang, I get on my knees and crawl through the wind until I reach Mr. Kramer and Jake. I take one of his arms and help Jake pull. When I look over at Lindsey, I see she's crying, so once I know Jake has Mr. Kramer safely under the table, I move toward her.

"It's okay, just a little wind," I say, putting my arms around her. She's shaking and staring forward, her arms still above her head. "Let's get under here with the rest of them until it passes."

But I don't really think this is going to pass. The wind is actually growing stronger, knocking over trash cans and anything else not nailed to the ground. Luckily this old picnic table was cemented down, so it's shaking a bit, but at least it's not taking flight.

Finally under the table, we're all huddled together. Mr. Kramer looks like he's sleeping, but I think he's unconscious. Jake has one arm around him and the other around Krystal. Lindsey and I are sitting cross-legged. I still have my arm around her, and she's still crying.

We all sit like that, watching in awe as what seemed like a little windstorm quickly changes course.

Everything is flying around, from tree branches to screened doors. The wind makes this howling sound that echoes in my ears. It's whisking around and around until suddenly there's loud thunder from above. I can't see the sky, but I can see the streaks of lightning that drop down from it. Each streak breaks something in its path, a huge oak tree splits in half, a house down the road catches fire, a car explodes.

Now I'm shaking, trying really hard not to get hysterical. Lindsey's about to fall completely apart. I hear Krystal scream and Jake trying to console her. My chest fills with something like a yell but I bite it back, hoping it doesn't break free.

Then alongside the crackling lightning bolts comes a thin stream of what looks like smoke. In a few seconds I see my assessment is wrong, it's not smoke, it's a funnel cloud, and it begins to spread.

Opening its mouth like a wide yawn, it grows bigger and bigger until its tip touches the ground. Then everything in its wake is sucked up. Houses. Cars. Utility poles. Everything.

Above us, the table rattles like it's going to take flight soon. We're out in the open with no protection. I look around quickly, but there's nothing to hold on to except each other. Now I do scream because that funnel is getting closer, and we have nowhere to run.

A lot of things are running through my mind: will I ever see Antoine again? Where's Casietta and Mouse? The school, Krystal's parents, our lives, my shoes. It's a hodgepodge of stuff just whirling around like the wind and debris, and I figure this is what's meant by your life passing before your eyes. My heart's hammering in my chest. Lindsey is openly sobbing, and I keep a tight hold on her, rocking back and forth, trying to project a fearlessness I don't really possess.

Then the funnel stops, like just stops right in front of us. It's still twirling, the wind is still blowing viciously, but the funnel itself isn't moving. The howling increases, but in between, I'd swear I can hear laughter. His laughter. It grows louder and louder.

Within the funnel I can see chairs and trees, trash and cars, dogs and light poles, all twirling around in the cloudy mass. Then I see something that has to be the least expected of them all. Shadowy figures, tall, thin, slinkylike and black. They're breaking from the funnel as if the huge cloud is simply spitting them out.

Shaking, I look over at Jake and Krystal to see if they're

seeing the same thing. From their gaping mouths and virtually still bodies, I think they are.

Dozens of them break free of the funnel, moving about the earth without actually touching the ground. They split up, all going in different directions, as if following some type of leader that I can't see.

"Wh-what...is...it?" I stutter.

"I don't know!" Krystal screams.

Jake just shakes his head.

The laughter grows louder. "You won't win," the deep voice says.

Then, as if in the blink of an eye, the funnel is gone. The wind is still, and the sky is bright blue with the sun blazing all its golden glory.

We all stay under the table, shaking, reeling, trying to make sense of what we've just seen.

Knowing it means only one thing. This battle has just taken a serious turn, and we might just be outnumbered.

# twenty-six

"Oh, you're awake. Finally."

My mother is sitting on the side of my bed. Her face looks tight, maybe because her hair's pulled back and sprayed stiffly. From what I can see, she's wearing slacks and a yellow blouse. Today is casual. She has on her pearls—the single strand choker and the stud earrings.

And she's holding my hand.

"I've been waiting and waiting. Casietta said you were probably very tired. But even so, you've been asleep for hours."

She's still talking as I turn my head and look out the window. It's daylight, which means I slept all night. Cool. I didn't think I would. Not after that tornado and those things that came from it. I just knew I was going to have nightmares. But I actually feel very rested.

I'm hungry, too.

"Is Casietta around?" I ask in a dry voice.

For a minute, my mother just blinks at me, like I've spoken in some foreign language. I rethink what I said and hope that wasn't actually the case.

But then she clears her throat and says, "I'm here, Sasha. For whatever you need, I am here."

Yeah, right, okay.

"Where's Casietta?" I ask again.

Now she actually looks a little hurt. I try to sit up. "I, um, wanted to see if she'd bring me some fruit or something. Can you call her?"

"She's gone," she says rather abruptly.

"Gone?" I push back the sheets and attempt to get out of the bed. "Gone where?"

She doesn't answer right away because she's trying to keep me in the bed. "Now, you lie still a little longer. You rush out of bed, you'll get a headache."

She doesn't know I'm already getting a headache. "Where is Casietta?" I ask, plopping back down on my pillows.

My mother huffs and brushes off the front of her blouse like having to touch me or assist me has caused her some discomfort.

"If you must know right this minute, she's gone back to Argentina."

"What? Why?"

"Some disagreement between her and your father. Marvin didn't think she was doing her job as well—probably because of her age. I don't really know. I'll be interviewing new prospects next week. But for right now, would you like me to get you anything?"

Yeah, I'd like my guardian back. I'd like Casietta. I don't speak because I don't know what to say. I'm totally speechless. What will happen to me now? If Casietta has been guarding me all this time, what will happen now that she's gone?

"She's been with me forever and she does a great job," I start to say, but my mother quickly puts up a hand to quiet me.

"It's done. Your father has decided."

"And when he decides it's done, no questions asked." I hear the words and wonder if I should take them back. But I don't want to, this is so unfair.

My mother is quiet, and for the first time, I realize she's sad. "Casietta was my friend, too, Sasha. But she had to go. We'll get along fine without her."

Just before she stands and turns away, I see her bottom lip quiver. Whatever I was going to say next is stalled.

So Casietta is gone, and there are more dark things slinking around on earth. This is just great.

"Where's Dad now?" I ask out of sheer curiosity. I haven't seen him since I gave him the ultimatum to leave Jake alone. I guess I should have had the foresight to add Casietta in that deal as well.

"He had a business trip, went into the city last night."

Last night, before or after I was brought home by the paramedics, I wonder.

We're all okay, but after we climbed from beneath the table all shaken up, Jake's dad thought it was best if we got checked out.

"So it's just you and me in the house?"

"For a couple of days. Like I said, I'll be interviewing next week for a replacement for Casietta."

"Nobody can replace her," I say quickly.

My mother nods her head as if she was about to say the same thing.

"I'll go down and fix you something to eat. You just sit here and gather your strength."

"I'm going to school," I say, pushing back the sheets and swinging my legs from the bed.

Standing at the door, my mother just nods. "Okay. I'll let Mr. Lycanian know."

And then she's gone and I'm alone.

I spend a few seconds thinking, and then I realize there's no point. I don't know what happened between my father and

Casietta and may never know. But I have to deal with the here and now—with these things that came with last night's storm and with the relationship I've left hanging.

"What's up with you? You look like you've lost your BFF," Krystal says, dropping down to sit on the school steps beside me after school. She's got her books in her arms and her purse on her shoulder. She's wearing jeans and a white blouse with blue stripes. Her hair's hanging around her shoulders, and for the first time in days she looks normal.

I just shrug and then ask the question that's been bugging me all day where she's concerned. "Have you talked to Franklin?"

She shakes her head negatively but doesn't look at me. "His cell phone is disconnected and their house phone just rings. There's no car in their driveway and there was a fill-in doing the weather this morning. I think they're gone."

"Sounds like it," I say, not sure how she's taking that bit of news. "But what about your vision? You saw Mr. Bryant showing what's on that flash drive to a room full of people. We still need to know exactly what he knows."

"As long as he's out of Lincoln I don't think we're gonna make that happen." She sighs. "I heard your dad's out of town, too."

"How'd you hear that?"

"Alyssa was in the hallway bragging about this new club and how she's helping the Carringtons but that the plans would have to wait until Mr. Carrington returned from his business trip."

Wow, talk about news traveling fast. I didn't even think anybody in school would care about that little tidbit of information, but I guess if it was one of Alyssa's flunkies listening, they care about whatever she has to say.

"Listen, about the Alyssa situation. My mom pushed me and her together. I didn't volunteer to work with her in any way."

Krystal just waves a hand in my direction. "Don't worry about it. It's over."

"I really hope it is because I had nothing to do with the way she was treating you. I'd never do that."

"I know," Krystal says, and then she does look over at me. "When me and Jake talked about it, he made me see that it wasn't something you'd do. I guess I was just trippin' about the Franklin thing, too, so I needed somebody to take it out on."

"For the record," I say with a small smile, "I don't think Franklin had any control over the stuff he was doing. I mean, if he was trying to take your eyes, maybe his had already been taken. And like Jake's granddad said, the eyes are the windows to the soul. I think he really liked you."

"Yeah, well, I'm not looking forward to the love arena anytime soon."

I chuckle. "I hear that," I answer, looking out toward the parking lot instead.

"Why are you sitting out here alone? Where's Mouse?"

"Running late. I was going to go somewhere after school that I didn't want him to know about, but my plans changed."

"You were going to go out with Antoine?"

I didn't think Krystal had been paying attention to my issues with Antoine. For weeks she'd been so busy avoiding me, or casting me dirty looks. Anyway, I really do need to talk about this thing with him. And since I don't have a BFF— the thought of Alyssa's offer to fill that position still makes me want to hurl—I guess confiding in a Mystyx will do just fine.

Over the weekend I'd sent him like four texts, but he didn't respond to any of them. So last night, just before I'd gone over to Jake's, I'd called him. He didn't answer his cell. I called his house and Aunt Pearl said he was taking a nap. I didn't believe that excuse at all.

"He's so pissed at me right now."

"Why? What'd you do?"

"It's more like what I didn't do."

"And that is?"

I sigh heavily. It's one thing to internalize your faults and mistakes. It's another thing entirely voicing them so that the words are forever out in the universe. "I didn't stand up for us. I should have been proud to be with him, proud of our relationship. But I wasn't. I wasn't brave enough to go against the rules."

Krystal chuckles. "Really? Are you serious?"

I look at her questioningly.

"You've done nothing but break rules since I've met you and you were probably doing it long before then."

"No, I haven't."

Krystal puts her books on the step beneath us, then starts to count off on her fingers. "First, you're friends with Jake, like best friends with him. He's from the Tracks and you're a Richie. Breaking the rules. Then you start hanging out with me, the crazy new girl who sees ghosts and breaks out the windows in her house. Breaking the rules. You ignore Alyssa and tell your parents you won't help them promote a club that excludes people. And I'm not even mentioning how you saved Jake's house."

I hold my hand up to stop her next words. "Don't say it. I know, breaking the rules."

She laughs. "See?"

I can't help it, I smile, too. It feels nice to have a girl to talk to about this stuff.

"Yeah, but I wasn't going to let Mouse take me to Antoine's house today. I was going to catch the bus with him."

"And he didn't like that?"

"He's ignoring me. The last thing he said to me was that he thinks I'm still hiding our relationship."

"Are you?"

I lean back, resting my elbows on the cement. Tilting my head back, I look up into the bright sunny sky. The warm rays feel good against my skin. "I just don't want any interference, you know? It's like I have this one good thing that supernatural powers and silly prejudices can't touch. Or rather, I don't want them to touch."

"So you think if you keep it quiet, it'll stay good?"

"I was hoping."

"I don't know the answer, Sasha. But I'm willing to bet you're not going to figure it out sitting here chatting it up with me."

We both laugh at that and a few minutes later I'm walking back inside the school building, heading to where I know Antoine is still hanging out.

I'm actually the one looking for Antoine this time. I can't believe it. But he hasn't returned any of my calls or my texts. I know he's still pissed about that day last week when he called and wanted to meet up. I couldn't tell him why I couldn't go out with him, and he immediately jumped to the wrong conclusion. I wasn't trying to hide being with him, I just had other things to do.

I wonder if I'll ever be able to tell him about my powers. Maybe we'll get rid of the threat before I have to. At any rate, I at least need to talk to him to clear the air. I just need to find him first.

I see him at the end of the hallway standing near some

lockers with his fellow hip-hop crew—or friends, I should say. Antoine is constantly telling me the guys he hangs with aren't as bad as everybody thinks they are. I think it's time I start taking those words to heart. So I take a deep breath and keep right on walking towards them. Two of the guys see me coming and nudge Antoine, who finally looks up at me with a none-too-pleased look on his face.

I'm nervous, but I'm trying desperately not to show it. My jeans suddenly feel too tight, my legs stiff as they move. I swallow deeply just as I come up on them, and my lips tremble into a smile. "Hi," I finally manage in a small voice.

"Hey, cutie." The one called Fats, with his super-round stomach and even rounder face, speaks to me first. He's not a bad-looking guy with his root-beer toned skin and silver-gray eyes. His hair is in cornrows, and he has an earring in his left ear. His clothes are super neat, jeans cuffed at the ankles and a New York Giants jersey. "What brings you all the way down here to our corner of the world?" he asks jovially.

I guess this is their corner of the world since there appears to be nobody down this end of the hall but them. Turning around briefly, I see farther down the opposite side the kids have done much the same as they do in the cafeteria. Three or four Goths stand near the water fountain, while a big cluster of jocks are close to the door. Everyone finding their kind and sticking with them.

Turning back to face Fats, I think it's even crazier than before. "I need to talk to Antoine," I say a little louder than I'd been speaking previously. I don't want there to be any doubts about why I'm here or who I'm here to see.

Antoine does what he always does, slips his hands into his pockets and just stares at me. He doesn't say a word.

The one they call Trigga smiles at me. He's taller than

all of us and rail-thin like he was born specifically to play basketball.

"Oooohhh, you wanna talk to Twan. Well, go ahead and talk to him."

I look right up at him and say, "Alone."

To Fats this must be one helluva joke because he starts to laugh like I'm a comedian onstage. Antoine just nods his head and they both get his message.

In a few seconds we're alone. He's still standing a short distance from me, and his facial expression hasn't changed.

"I think…ah…there was a misunderstanding the other day," I begin. It's unnerving that he's not moving or saying anything. I'm trying to gauge his reaction to me being here, but he's making it very difficult.

"What I mean is, when you called me I really did have something to do. I couldn't just drop it and come meet you."

He remains silent for a few more seconds, and I feel like I'm drowning. I don't know what else to say, what else to do. Should I just walk away, leave him alone as he seems to want me to do? Or should I stay and say my piece? I think I already have, but it doesn't seem to have helped.

"Well, that's all I wanted to say." I turn and am getting ready to leave when I feel a hand on my shoulder.

"You could have just said you were busy and you'd call me back later."

The sound of his voice warms me inside, and I slowly turn back around to face him. "I was in a hurry and so much was going on." I sigh. "Yeah, I could have."

"But you didn't. It was like you were brushing me off one final time."

I'm shaking my head negatively. "No. It definitely wasn't like that."

"But you don't want to tell me what it was like?"

"I just did. I had something else to do, so I couldn't meet you. It wasn't that I didn't want to be with you the way you made it seem."

He shrugs. "I can't really tell with you."

I swallow and realize I'm going to have to put it all out there. "I know I've been kind of on the fence with this whole thing, but I just had some stupid hang-ups about us being together. I'm not ashamed of you or of us, together, I mean. I'm really not."

"Prove it," he says, and the corner of his mouth kind of lifts into a smile.

I don't really know how to prove this to him. Or rather, I don't know what he expects me to do. But on impulse, I take another step closer to him. I push up on my tiptoes because he's taller than me, and I kiss him. Right there in the hallway with the after-school kids still hanging around, I, Sasha Carrington, supposed Richie, kiss Antoine Watson, supposed bad boy, right on the lips.

His smile grows bigger, then he wraps his arms around me and kisses me right back.

And for this one moment in time, I feel like all is well.

# twenty-seven

*Five Weeks Later*

It's the last day of school.

Weeks have gone by since the storm, since we saw those inky black things come from the funnel. I haven't traveled to the Majestic, nor have I spoken to Fatima the Messenger.

Krystal hasn't had any visions about Mr. Bryant and his research, and Jake seems to be coming out of his funk. Lindsey's a little touch-and-go sometimes, but I can tell she's really trying to fit in with us. I think she already does.

Casietta's still gone. I've written her two letters but haven't received any response. At some point, I guess I'll give up. My dad came back from his business trip, and he's even more quiet than ever. I don't care. I don't have much to say to him anyway. My mom's been a little weird, coming into my room a lot, acting like she just wants to talk. She's still on the health food kick, and she still loves her committees, but I think something's changed with her since Casietta left.

Antoine is my boyfriend. Yes, it's official. He even came to dinner at my house last week. It was just me, him and my mother, but that was just fine.

I wonder if the Darkness has moved on.

Then I look up as we're sitting in the cafeteria and see it.

At the far end, where the exit doors are, there are two

windows on the side. The sun is shining through every other window in the cafeteria. Except these two.

The panes have grown dark.

"Ah, guys," I say to Krystal and Jake. Lindsey's sitting right beside me, so I tap her on the leg.

They all follow my gaze.

Through the dark window panes, a thick gooey goop is coming. It's trailing down the walls, touching the floor, then sliding across like a trail of blood.

We don't move, don't say a word, but the heat at my side and the sight of Krystal rubbing the back of her neck says we're thinking along the same lines.

The Darkness is back.

# epilogue

I never knew there were different levels of Hell. Then again, I had no idea there was such a thing as demons and gods and souls to be taken. Life for me has existed around my father's incessant rantings about storm patterns and excess energy. Good and bad seemed like basic common sense. Do good things, don't do bad things. Everybody learned that as a kid. Some experts call it discipline.

Yet this is different. This dark, cold place I find myself in. Oh yeah, the burning in the fires of hell theory might be true, but not on the level I'm in at the moment. Where I'm at, my breath is like frost, my fingers already numb, even though I think I've only been here a couple of minutes.

The move happened quick, like a flash of light. One minute I was with Krystal—ah, remembering her touch warms me a bit. Let's hope that memory lasts, I've got a feeling I'm going to need some nice hot thoughts to get me through this. For about the time it took me to blink or inhale, I was gone from Krystal's arms and dropped here. In Hell.

How do I know I'm in Hell?

Because there is no feeling, good or bad. There is no end. I'm like on this ledge, and if I take a step, I'll fall, but I don't know where I'll fall to. Probably another level but I can't see it. There's nothing down there but pitch black. The ledge only looks like it goes so far, then there's nothing.

I'm all alone.

Yes, this is definitely Hell.

Another reason I know I'm in Hell—all the skulls and other dead body parts that seem frozen into the wall behind me. They look like somebody scared the hell out of them—no pun intended. Or scared them directly into Hell—either way it's not a cool sight.

And while I should be afraid, should be wondering how I came to be here and what will happen to me next, I'm not.

I don't even jump when icy cold fingers touch my shoulder. And when I look down, I see bones, finger bones, but bones nonetheless, resting on my left shoulder as if waiting for me to acknowledge them. So I turn slowly, being extra careful not to let my foot go over the edge and fall into the dark oblivion.

My heart should have been beating fast with fear, but I don't think my heart's in there anymore. Actually, it doesn't feel like I have anything on the inside. No thumping, no movement, just nothing. Kind of like what it looks like to fall off this ledge.

Of course there's a body attached to the bone fingers. It's wearing all black—how appropriate. The robe seems long and the hood is lifted, and there's no face—like the pictures of a reaper. But if I'm in Hell, I'm already dead, so there's no need for a reaper to come for me.

"Come. He waits." The reaperlike thing has a deep voice that echoes off the nothing environment and almost busts my eardrum.

When I don't make a move, the bone fingers grab me up by the collar. My feet are dangling in the air now, no skinny ledge and no falling into nothing. Better yet, reaperlike thing has just sprouted wings from his back, and the next thing I know, we're both lifted into the cold air of darkness. The wings are huge and gray-black, flapping wildly, creating a loud clacking sound and an even cooler breeze.

There's just more dark for as far as I can see, but reaperlike flying thing is moving quick, as if it knows exactly where to go and how to get there.

Again, I'm not afraid but figure that'll change soon enough.

★ ★ ★ ★ ★

# QUESTIONS FOR DISCUSSION

1. Have you ever been asked to choose friends based on their status or how much money they had? If so, how did you handle it?

2. Do you think Sasha should be more honest with Antoine about how she feels about him?

3. Sasha can astral project to another plane called the Majestic. Do you believe another world or dimension, besides Earth, exists?

4. The Majestic is home to magical beings. How do you think the knowledge of this place will affect the Mystyx?

5. Sasha unknowingly hurts Krystal and Jake's feelings by snubbing them for her wealthy friends. How do you think she could have handled the situation better?

6. Greek mythology is prevalent in modern-day astrology. Have you ever felt that the sun or the moon exuded some type of power over your actions and behavior? How?

7. Because Lindsey reveals herself as one of the Mystyx, Sasha wonders if there is a particular reason that Lindsey showed up in Lincoln. Do you think it's connected to the battle they're preparing for or just a coincidence?

8. What ways do you think the Mystyx can use their powers to fight the Darkness? What are the limits of their powers and how do you think it will affect their ability to battle evil?

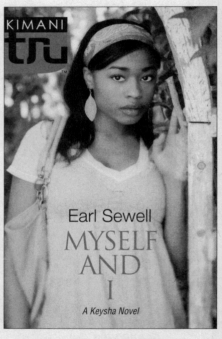